the buddha bar

THE BUDDHA BAR
A NOVEL

JOSEPH RIDGWELL

Ternary Editions
New York

SECOND EDITION

The first edition of *The Buddha Bar* was published in 2011 by Blackheath Books of England in an edition limited to one hundred copies.

ISBN-13:   978-1-937073-73-2

TERNARY
EDITIONS
29 Sugar Hill Road
North Salem, NY 10560

www.ternaryeditions.com

This book is dedicated to all the backpackers and lonely travelers of the world dreaming of never going home.

1.

It was a bed made out of bamboo and I was naked. A repetitive noise could be heard. Awake now, I lay there listening. It was the sound of chopping. Each chop occurred at regular intervals. I opened my eyes. Where was I? Total disorientation. I brushed aside a pink mosquito net. It was a beach hut situated on a tiny Malaysian island.

I jumped into a pair of ripped shorts and stepped outside. Croatian Karl was squatted on a rickety porch, knife held above his head. I'd hooked up with him in Kuala Lumpur. He walked over and started talking to me as I sat in an airport bar, drinking a cold beer and doing nothing.

Karl lowered the knife and a slice of coconut husk fizzed past my left ear. Lined up on the porch were three skilfully guillotined coconuts. The decapitated coconuts and the size of the blade in Karl's hand gave me food for thought. What if he was a serial killer? I studied his eyes, you can always tell by the eyes. His eyes were blue and friendly.

Karl looked up from the squat position.

'Ah, Joseph, you are finally awake. Would you like some coconut milk?'

'Don't mind if I do.'

I picked up one of the coconuts and took a sip. The liquid was warm and tasted vile.

'This island is one big coconut grove,' said Karl, as I spat liquid into some jungle to my left.

'Yeah,' I said, wiping my mouth.

Karl raised his arm. 'You know coconut milk and meat are very nutritious. It's possible to live predominantly off a diet of coconuts - breakfast, lunch, dinner -a good way to save money.'

I placed my hands on hips, akimbo style. 'Live off a diet of coconuts and coconuts alone, are you on drugs?'

Karl lowered his arm ... and swish, another piece of coconut fizzed off to the right.

'All the minerals and vitamins we need are right here inside this husk.'

2.

We spent the rest of the day at the beach, chilling in a couple of dirty hammocks that were sheltered from the terrible Malay sun by shady mangrove trees. We swung languidly to and fro.

'Ever been to the Adriatic?' asked Karl.

I shook my head.

'Ever been to Croatia?'

'Huh?'

Karl leapt out of his hammock and paced the sand.

'Never been to the Adriatic or Croatia. Why not?'

'Dunno.'

'You should know. It's without doubt the most beautiful country in the whole world. And, what's more, Opatija is the most beautiful place in the whole world.'

'Really, are you not a little biased?'

'The beauty of my homeland cannot be denied my friend. Picture this scene: long Mediterranean summers - balmy nights - fragrant lemon groves - olive trees - green rolling hills – mountains - white washed houses - fishing boats bobbing in sparkling Adriatic waters.'

'So when are we going?'

Karl pointed towards the sea with a wide expansive gesture. I gazed at the view, coral beach, turquoise sea and endless blue sky ... a tranquil scene akin to paradise.

'That shit, beautiful as it is' said Karl, 'is nothing compared to the beauty of Opatija and its women.'

'Its women?'

'Why of course, the women of Croatia are without doubt the most beautiful women in the whole world, and the girls of Opatija the best of a magnificent bunch!'

'Let's go there now,' I demanded.

'Forget it. First I have to save money, for without money there is no life to speak of for me in Opatija. No, I will not return until I have saved some cash.'

'But how the fuck ya gonna save some cash out here?

'By signing on as a steward on a cruise ship in the Philippines, what else? Then, when I've saved enough money, I'll return home and start life over again.'

Working on a cruise ship was not my idea of a lucrative career move. However, Karl was full of positive vibes.

'Do not worry,' he said confidently, 'once I've re-established myself in my homeland, I'll invite you over so you can see for yourself.'

I walked to where the sea met the beach and stepped into the green water.

'Don't forget that invite,' I called out, just as the sun sank below the horizon and turned the tropical sky yellow, orange and, finally, a magnificent, opulent purple

3.

Karl told me about the party by leaving a note in the hut. It was dark by this time. After reading the letter I got dressed, sprayed myself all over with industrial strength mosquito repellent, and strolled along a jungle path. The winding path led to the other side of the island and a collection of ramshackle restaurants and bars.

I found Karl plotted up in the Green Lizard bar, constructing a pyramid with some playing cards. He was the only customer.

'Look,' he said showing me the pack of cards, 'if you buy four Tiger beers you get a free pack of cards.'

'Groovy.'

As there were a few hours to kill before the party we sat chatting about this and that, building card pyramids and boozing. Ah, the joys of travel, the endless hours with nothing to do, or how to kill time. Then, just as Karl constructed a record breaking twelve level pyramid, the sound of bass heavy music distracted him at the vital moment. The structure collapsed.

I drained my beer. 'Must be the beach party.'

Karl looked at the scattered cards in disgust.

'Bullshit, I would have made it.'

'Come on, let's check out the party.'

We walked slowly along a sandy path. It was a hot night accompanied by the slightest sea breeze, just strong enough to rustle palm fronds high above. The smell of the tropics was all around, heavy, luxuriant and sensual, and in the velvet sky a few silver stars twinkled.

The beach party was already underway. Groups of travellers congregated in little camps on the sand, fires leapt in the dark, and in front of a makeshift sound system twenty or thirty people danced awkwardly to muffled techno.

We meandered along, observing the scene. There was a sand sculptor at work, a circle of travellers watching his progress by candlelight, and beyond some enterprising locals patrolled the shore armed with ice and booze filled buckets.

The most popular drink amongst the travellers was a cheap local whiskey known as monkey juice. A picture of an orangutan was labelled on each bottle. It was pure firewater. Me and Karl sat cross-legged on the beach, guru style, and waited for a happening.

Eventually a couple of female travellers approached. They were holding a bottle of monkey juice each. After some stilted intros we talked for a while. Probably out of boredom more than anything, Karl made a move.

'Have ever been to Croatia?'

'No,' said the boozy girls.

'You haven't?' said Karl, 'well you should, and if you go you must visit Opatija. Opatija is my village and it is the most beautiful...'

As this scene was played out I made a discreet exit, mumbling something about going back to the hut to fetch a torch. Instead I brought six tiger beers from one of the bucket men and found a secluded section of beach far from the party. I sat down on a large rock and gazed out to sea. As I wondered what to do with the rest of my life a pale blue moon appeared from behind a silver cloud.

I stared at the moon and back to the sea. Almost twenty-eight and I hadn't even managed to master a trade. Back home, people of my generation were getting their lives in order: building successful careers, buying stuff, climbing the first rungs of the property ladder. Some were even rearing the next generation born to die.

Fuck it. Maybe I was depressed or something. I'd fought all my life to be a non-conformist, but it was a difficult path to follow and without money almost impossible. 'Where are the rebels?' I asked the moon. The only sound was the waves crashing on the rocks below my rock. An ethereal moon glade flashed across the surface of the water. Some enchanted evening for someone, somewhere.

I entered a coconut grove and weaved between the swaying palms. Something had to turn up. I leaned against a trunk, contemplated ways to postpone my return to the UK and sipped my beer.

A loud swishing noise followed by two dull thuds interrupted my future life ruminations. It was a large coconut. I looked up. Bunches of shadowy coconuts nestled at the top of each palm tree.

I rolled the fallen coconut under my foot; it was massive, bigger than my head. If a coconut of similar dimensions scored a direct hit it would have killed me outright. Freaked, I decided to get out of the coconut grove and head back to the party.

In my absence the beach had transformed into a battlefield, with casualties of the merriment scattered everywhere or crashed out on the sand. Some stragglers wandered about disjointedly and a few hardcore freaks huddled in refugee camps around glowing fires. The sand sculptor had disappeared and someone had walked all over his sculpture, so now it was just the ruin of a sculpture, and the whole scene reminded me of death.

I looked at the bodies asleep on the beach. Some clutched monkey juice bottles to their chests like prized possessions, or comfort blankets. That could've been me crashed out on the beach, I reflected, or maybe swimming naked in the sea with a beautiful girl. I conducted a search for Karl amongst the wounded and dying, but was unable to find him anywhere. He was missing and the party was over.

I found the jungle path and returned to my hut. Noises from within the flimsy structure encouraged me to open the door with caution. The occupants didn't notice. Karl's white arse moved up and down robot style and the girl's legs dangled in the air like the pins of a strange fleshy puppet. I casually smoked a cigarette, but as they manoeuvred awkwardly into a 69 position, I closed the door as quietly as possible and sauntered towards the seashore.

At the shore was a small wooden jetty. I walked to the end of the jetty and sat down. In the morning it would be time to leave the country. If Karl wanted to come, all well and good; but if not, I'd still leave. I watched a rising pink creep across the horizon and waited for God to show his face.

4.

I awoke to a luxuriant yellow spreading across the bay. The light illuminated a shipwreck on a distant sand bank; a boat so rotted and bleached by other suns it resembled a skeleton. On the beach a mangy wild dog trotted across the sand, nose to ground. It stopped, pointed its snout skywards, and growled. The plaintive growl reverberated like a discordant dog blues, a comforting, reassuring sound. It was time to leave the country.

Back at the hut Karl and the blonde girl remained fast asleep in bed. The girl's breasts were uncovered, a nice size, just over a handful, with large aureoles and thick brown nips. Really I should charge her a night's board, I thought, but the view and free sex show turned me against the idea. It was worth £1.50 just to see it.

I stomped around the hut. 'Come on, get up, you're missing a beautiful day outside,' I bellowed.

Karl adopted a squinty eyed look.

'Where the hell did you get to last night?'

'Where the hell did I get to? I came back last night to crash and found the boudoir otherwise occupied!'

Karl smiled awkwardly, while the girl slipped under the sheet.

'Sorry Joseph, oh God I'm never, ever, going to drink that monkey juice again, unbelievable!'

'I'm going to Thailand, wanna come?'

Karl didn't even blink.

'Yes, yes, for sure, that's what I was thinking of doing anyway.'

What a result. Despite a predilection for travelling alone it didn't feel right leaving Karl behind. It felt like the time with my new friend had only just begun and we still had a few adventures to experience together.

After Karl got rid of the girl we caught the next available ferry to the mainland. The boatman fiddled with the petrol engine. On the fifth attempt the engine spluttered into life and the vessel chugged across the strait.

We sat at the back of the boat and gazed at the island.

'You gonna keep in contact with that bird?'

Karl pulled out a strip of paper, upon which the girl's email address was written. He screwed it up and headed it into the sea.

'Nah.'

The paper floated on the water for a while, before disappearing under the surface. I watched the island grow smaller and smaller. I'd never go there again. Some flying fish broke the surface, appearing either side of the boat's bow, and skating away at right angles.

'You know, I'm glad to be leaving Malaysia,' said Karl.

'Me too,' I replied, but leaving meant a return to the UK was getting closer and closer, like some unavoidable date with destiny, a black cloud hovering ominously on the horizon.

5.

After crossing the Thai/Malay border we arrived at a pretty little town situated at the mouth of the Sang Som River, where the sluggish brown water flows between two huge limestone cliffs and out into the Andaman Sea. It was here that we decided to stay.

Across the road from the balcony of another cheap guesthouse was a food market. The smells emanating from the cluster of stalls made me instantly hungry. As Karl was asleep I didn't bother to wake him and walked over to the market by myself.

Situated beneath our room was a tour operator's shop staffed by four young girls. As I descended the stairs the girls all looked at me at the same time. It was slightly unnerving. Then one of them approached.

'Wha you name?' she asked.

I gave her the once over: pretty, large black eyes, waist length jet-black hair.

'Joseph.'

'Oh Jo-sep that nice name.'

'What's your name?'

'My name Mindi,' she announced dramatically, like her moniker deserved to be accompanied by a fanfare of trumpets. Then she slipped a petite arm in mine and commenced a well-rehearsed sales spiel.

'You wan ferry to island you buy ticket me. You wan Tiger Temple you buy ticket me. You wan elephant jungle ride you buy ticket me. You wan scuba diving you buy ticket me. You wan learn how cook Thai you buy ticket me. Anything you wan I get, an you buy ticket me.'

I extricated my arm and backed away.

'Sounds good, but right now I'm hungry. Maybe I'll buy some tickets tomorrow?'

'Yah, you eat now then buy ticket me.'

'Yeah, sure.'

In the market I wandered from stall to stall studying the delicacies on offer with hungry eyes. There was plenty of fried fish, squid, and other fresh seafood. I approached one of the stalls, but was met with a look of incomprehension when I tried to order in English. The cook shrugged his broad shoulders, flipped something over in a frying pan, wiped a greasy hand across the front of his dirty apron, and did nothing.

I looked around for help. The pretty shop girl was watching with interest. She had one hand on her hip, and even from a distance oozed sex appeal. There was a faint stirring in my groin region, it wasn't much, but I felt it.

I indicated for the girl to come over, but she just poked her tongue out and walked back inside the shop. Cheeky, I thought, and acting on a whim strode over to the shop in a purposeful manner. The girl and I eyeballed each other.

'Wha you wan?' she asked.

The girl possessed beautiful eyes, eyes like the dead of night. They reminded me of the song Spanish Eyes, but the girl wasn't Spanish and Thai eyes didn't sound so good so I forgot about the song.

'I need help ordering some food. That guy over there doesn't speak English and I don't speak Thai.'

The girl tapped a pencil on the table. 'Busy I.'

I looked around. The shop was empty. It felt like a challenge and money seemed the only way to meet it head on. I flashed a wad of cash at the other shop girls. The sight of money excited them and an argument ensued. I split the money into three separate wads.

'Listen, why don't you all help?'

The girls smiled like small children until the other girl barked in Thai, silencing them in an instant.

'Busy also,' said Mindi sweetly, who was evidently the leader on this particular trip.

I rubbed my chin, said nothing, and returned to the food stall. Fuck her, I thought. The fat man saw me coming and smiled like an old friend. I decided to be more assertive with my ordering. I pointed at several items on the menu, rubbed my stomach, made munching noises with my mouth, and flashed the cash. This time the man got the idea and began chucking ingredients into a huge frying pan.

18

I brought a large Singha beer and sat at a plastic table. After five or ten minutes the cook began placing dishes on the table until seventeen were in front of me. To complement the food he added five tiny saucers filled with spices and dips, and a dispenser of chillies.

I looked at all the food in wonder. There was far more than what I'd ordered or thought I'd ordered, but I remained silent and formed my eyes into slits, viewing the situation as a tremendous challenge.

I paid for the meal, gave a tip, and prepared to eat. The cook smiled and said something in Thai, which I took to mean bon appetite. I pulled a serviette from a plastic dispenser and tucked it into the neck of my tee shirt with a certain flourish. I looked to the guesthouse across the road. The three deputies watched my every move.

I motioned them over with a wave of the hand and they smiled and looked to their leader. Mindi stopped what she was doing and glared at me. Eventually she slapped her hand on the desk and waved the three girls away. They ran over laughing and smiling.

'You eat all?' said one, gesturing to the multitude of dishes.

'Yep, unless you want to help,' I said, nonchalantly.

The girls exchanged knowing looks.

'No, we wan you eat, we think no possible.'

I glanced over my shoulder. The cook flipped something in his giant frying pan, in my mind daring me to finish all the food he had prepared.

'Not possible a?' I told the girls with a brave face, 'well check this out!'

Then I got started. By the fifth dish a crowd had gathered. I acknowledged the onlookers with a confident wave. After the ninth dish I ordered another large Singha beer and replaced the food-splattered serviette with a fresh one. I winked at the girls and gave the cook the thumbs up.

It soon became a battle of wills. I felt like Paul Newman in the boiled egg scene from the film Cool-Hand Luke. I went into tunnel vision mode, stuffing the food into my mouth, and taking large swigs of beer.

After the twelfth dish my belly tightened. The food rose from my stomach to my neck, and beyond. After the fourteenth dish I became a madman. My head was ready to burst, my eyes bulged out, the sweat poured off in torrents, and my belly assumed pregnant proportions. I called out for more beer, I called out for more chilli, I said brilliant things the girls didn't understand, yet bravely soldiered on

Finally, when the seventeenth dish disappeared with the other sixteen, I emitted the world's loudest burp and collapsed headfirst onto the table. There were yells of delight, cheering, an extended round of applause. I raised my head and blinked my eyes.

The girls fussed about my person, and although not feeling bad, I decided to milk the situation. As the crowd melted into the shadows I pointed feebly to the guesthouse, indicating they help me to my room.

Inside the shop I shrugged the girls from me and called out to their leader in a horse voice.

'Mindi?'

'Yah,'

'Tomorrow, me and my friend, we need tickets to the islands.'

'Yah, you wan now, you best price me!'

'No, no need, I'll buy them when I come down for breakfast,'

The girls were amazed.

'Tomorrow eat breakfast?'

'Of course, full English.'

'Fool English, wha that?'

I'll explain tomorrow,' I replied, and walked up the wooden staircase of the guesthouse like an ancient Zen master returning to his hermit's cave to meditate for a thousand years. On the way I bumped into a sleepy Karl emerging from the room.

'Unbelievable, what happened to you? You look like you just gone ten rounds with Klitschko,' he yawned.

'Just tired after eating.'

'Yes I'm hungry now, is there anywhere good to eat?

Despite the fact my stomach was about to explode, a mischievous thought entered my mind, dominating the others that resided there, the reasonable, boring, sensible types.

'Just tell the girls downstairs that you want exactly what I had from exactly the same place.'

Karl thanked me and I felt a pang of guilt, but that didn't last. I collapsed onto the bed, rubbed my huge stomach, and stared at a ceiling fan revolving above my head. Outside - voices.

'Wha mister Karl you wan same mister Jo-Jo, really?'

I closed my eyes.

6.

I woke early, sated and satisfied. Karl was not on his side of the bed. I found him downstairs, engaged in an animated conversation with one of the shop assistants. The pretty assistant gazed at him like he was a teen idol or movie star. In passing I heard the word Opatija mentioned. That man was obsessed.

I acknowledged Karl with a wave of the hand, found a table, and ordered a large Chang beer. Beer in hand, I observed the scene. Mindi was the epitome of dynamism, displaying impressive sales skills, combined with an abundance of natural charm. And when she put her arm around some male backpackers and fluttered her eyelashes, I experienced pangs of jealousy.

Dismissing the feelings, I switched attention to the other girls. They did a good impression of Mindi, but were nowhere near as accomplished. That's why Mindi was the leader. She was, by far, the most experienced sales person and she knew it.

Shortly Karl came over, carrying a large bowl of what looked like fruit yoghurt or something equally as vile. He glanced disapprovingly at the large bottle of beer I nursed in my hands, and shovelled the fruit shit into his mouth with healthy gusto.

'Right, we might as well fuck off today?' I said.

Karl swallowed what he was eating.

'Yes, doesn't seem much going on around here.'

'Pee Pee Island?'

'For sure.'

I tried to catch the eye of Mindi by waving, but she pretended to ignore me. That's weird, I thought. The other girls were busy serving a long line of customers. I tried to catch Mindi's eye again by using more and more expressive gestures.

Karl looked at me in a strange way.

'What are you doing?'

'I'm trying to buy a couple of tickets for the ferry.'

'Don't worry,' he said pointing at Mindi, 'she gave me a couple of tickets last night.'

'Really?'

'Yes, and unbelievable or what, she gave them for nothing. I think she like me.'

Again the jealousy pangs surfaced, but this news didn't surprise me because Karl was a handsome guy, who I could no way compete with in the looks stakes. 'What time does the ferry leave?'

'Every hour.'

'Let's catch the eleven o'clock boat.'

Just as we were about to leave I thanked Mindi for the free tickets.

'I no you free ticket, I give Karl,' she replied with a sneer.

This unnecessary comment wound me up, but I just bit my lip and walked away.

As we waited to board the ferry Mindi approached. Due to her unfriendly attitude I turned my back, intent on blanking her. She yanked me round by the tee shirt.

'How long stay island?'

'I don't know, why?'

Mindi dug a card out.

'Tomorrow I is-land, stay two day, you see me, me show you is-land.'

I examined the card. Written on the back was the address of a bar. I put the card in my pocket.

'Okay,' I said.

'When room on island, jus pay one night, maybe I free room, expensive hotel an you stay me.'

'Really?'

'Yah, really!'

It was then I remembered what she'd said when I'd tried to thank her for the ferry tickets. As she crossed the road an association of thoughts gave me an idea. I shouted out her name. Mindi turned around. I took out the card, and in a purposeful and conspicuous manner, tore it into many pieces and tossed them into the air.

Mindi threw a hand across her mouth and Karl looked at me like I'd gone crazy. Feeling revenge was mine, but also slightly evil, I picked up my backpack.

'Let's boogie,' I said sweetly.

'Unbelievable,' said Karl.

23

7.

On Pee Pee Island budget hotels were expensive. The only place we could afford was a small shack in a crowded street lined with a myriad of cheap guesthouses, souvenir shops, and tour agents. We glanced at the cramped surroundings of our new lodgings with long faces.

'We'll have to meet Mindi and see if she was serious about that offer of free accommodation,' I said.

'Yes, but for sure ripping up the card was a wrong move.'

That evening we walked out into another sultry tropical island night. Stars blinked in a midnight blue sky, a small round moon shone down, and the lovely sound of the ocean was all around. Signs and posters advertising a Muay Thai boxing event were everywhere. A team from Denmark were up against a local Thai team. Immediately Karl wanted in on the action.

The entrance to the bar was lit up with thousands of fairy lights, which gave it the feel of a grotto, and at the far end of the room stood a boxing ring. The place was rammed. Tourists mingled with locals, and in the middle of the room was an enormous wooden sculpture standing over twenty feet high.

I did a double check, but no my eyes had not been deceived. There it was, a huge golden phallus, a fantastic object glistening in the bright lights like some shining totem pole of debauchery. Karl and I sniggered like naughty schoolboys.

'Nearly as big as mine,' said Karl.

'Are you certain?'

'For sure.'

After admiring the impressive dick we ordered two beers, and compared the competing teams. Both sides were fit and athletic, young and lean of limb, in fact in the prime of physical life. After discussing possible victors, we decided to have a wager on the outcome, a small thousand baht winner takes all bet. As Muay Thai, or the Art of the Eight Limbs, is Thailand's national sport I went for the home team and Karl the Danes.

A master of ceremonies strode to the middle of the ring and introduced each fighter to the noisy crowd. The Danish fighter was the first to appear, a young, blonde, good-looking lanky fellow quickly followed by a dark, stocky, Thai fighter.

The Danish boy was dressed in a white silk robe with matching white leather boots. He pranced around the ring shadow boxing. Then he peeled off the robe to reveal a tanned torso and a pair of baby pink shorts. A group of Danish girls at ringside screamed like he was a member of a boy band or a pop idol.

'Over in round three,' I said confidently.

Despite the Dane's effeminate appearance, he was in peak condition and to the girls delight commenced showboating. He threw a few elegant demonstration punches and kicks, smiling and winking at the girls as he did. In contrast his opponent, dressed in black boots and black shorts, displayed an impenetrable Buddha-like exterior. I rested easy.

After the Ram Muay dance had been performed, and both fighters completed the Wai Kru, the action began.

Less than a minute in it became apparent that my man was going to win. Time and again he skilfully worked inside the Dane's superior reach and pounded him with ferocious combinations to body and head. It was brutal. The blonde could only survive by clinging desperately to his opponent, a tactic that forced the referee to intervene and separate the boxers.

I nudged Karl and smiled smugly. He was not amused. Whenever the Dane got in a decent punch or kick Karl raised a clenched fist and roared his approval, but by the end of the second round his stern expression had softened to that of a defeated man.

Sensing victory in the third the Thai fighter went in for the kill, and after a few devastating combinations, felled his opponent with a high kick to the chin. The Dane dropped to the canvas with a sickening thud and lay stricken on the canvas with a smile on his face, dreaming of his first love back in Copenhagen. His groupies gasped at the sight and buried their heads in the shoulders of their friends, afraid to look. As for the Thai crowd, they exchanged knowing glances as their man paraded the ring, arms aloft, savouring the short lived euphoria of victory.

The referee gave the obligatory count of ten in dramatic fashion, but he needn't have bothered. An act of futility. I slapped Karl on the back and said I'd get the beers in.

On my return the second bout was already underway, only this time it was a role reversal. The Thai fighter was tall, handsome, and graceful, while the Dane was short, ugly, and built like a brick shit house. This time around it was a much closer contest, and with the alcohol flowing freely, the crowd was more vocal and raucous. Pretty soon a buzzing atmosphere enveloped the bar.

The Thai fought in a graceful, almost beautiful style and rained down exquisite shots upon the Dane, who shrugged off each well-timed blow like they were nothing more than irritating flies.

As the fighting intensified the Danish contingent roared and the Danish girls screamed, the Thai contingent clapped politely, Karl raised his fist into the air, and I became distracted.

The only thing holding my interest was the bet, so to alleviate boredom I began looking around the pub. That's when I saw her, Mindi, standing at the bar with two Western men, laughing and smiling. I peered around the great golden dick. The threesome appeared to be getting along famously. It made me feel a little sick. I wondered who the men were and instantly hated them.

What I wanted to do was approach Mindi and talk to her. In fact I wanted to do more than that. I wanted to take her to my shack and make mad, passionate love to her all night long, followed by the breakfast of champions.

As I ruminated on how to achieve this glory aim my gaze returned to the boxing ring just as the Dane landed a peach of an uppercut, bang on the Thai fighter's chin. There was the impact of glove against skin and a small explosion of sweat burst into the air and rained down on ringside. The crowd roared, but from amongst the combined roar of a hundred throats I recognised the voice of Karl; seriously, that man could roar.

I turned my attention back to Mindi. Eventually she saw me and smiled. I returned her casual smile with a maniacal one. She eyed me oddly and resumed conversation with the two men.

I finished my beer and immediately got another, along with a whisky chaser. I downed the shot with the beer and repeated the trick. Then I swayed across the floor. The fairy lights blurred and the crowd roared, and the fighters fought, and I just about made it to the golden phallus without falling over.

It didn't take long to catch Mindi's eye. I motioned her over with a drunken wave of my arm. Mindi winked and poked out her tongue. God what a dream, a Thai dream for sure, but cheeky nonetheless. I thought about that tongue poking out of her mouth. I wanted to cut it out and display it to the patrons of the bar. And there was Karl.

'Are you okay?'

'Yeah, yes, who's winning?'

'One all.' Karl was sweating cobs and animated, 'would you like another beer?'

I showed him my full bottle.

The next fight was between two female fighters. The change of sex caught my attention, and for a few moments I forgot about Mindi and faced the ring. Just before the fight commenced Karl returned with the drinks and both of us concentrated on the outcome of the contest with that peculiar intensity only gamblers possess.

It was a good fight, although after the men it was like going from fast forward to slow motion; like watching the Men's tennis final followed by the Ladies'. The Thai girl out classed the Danish fighter and rained down flurries of gentle punches, but the blonde was gutsy and kept coming back for more punishment.

By the third round the girls were still battering each other, but once more my thoughts returned to Mindi. I retreated to my observation point behind the great golden dick. She was standing at the bar, alone. Drunk, I forget about everything else, and strode over, swaying and staggering all the way.

As I approached Mindi pulled a face and turned her back, but that wasn't going to stop me, I was out of control. I grabbed her arm and dragged her bodily towards the entrance of the bar. She yanked her arm away angrily.

'Hey, wha you do?'

'I want to talk to you outside.'

'Go away, me here my friend.'

I grabbed her arm again.

'Fuck your friend.'

I gained about five feet to the entrance before Mindi managed to extract her arm once more.

'Wha you do? Leave me alone.'

Some people noticed the altercation and stared.

'Listen I need to talk to you, it's important.'

Mindi eyed me suspiciously like she was trying to work me out, both confused and intrigued.

'Well?' I demanded.

'Okay, me give you five min, ba wait tell my friend, an remember I know all Thai people on island so no monkey business.'

I nodded and waited.

A few moments later Mindi reappeared.

'Wha you wan say?'

'Let's go to the beach.'

'No way, you tell here.'

I had to think of a tactic and fast. I decided to lie about the card- shredding incident.

'I want to explain why I ripped up your card, I think you got the wrong end of the stick.'

'Wong end stick, wha that?'

'Listen, just come for a walk along the beach an I'll explain everything.'

'You dwunk?'

I tried to look as sober as possible, which in the circumstances some would say was impossible, but I pulled it off before replying robot style.

'No I've just had a couple beers.'

'And wha about whis-kee, I see dwink whis-kee!'

'Oh yes and a whisky.'

'You tell on beach, I tell friend so he no way round.'

I nodded, turned on my heels, and looked up to the sky. It now seemed like a magic night and all my nerve-endings began to vibrate like a teenager about to embark on a first date.

8.

On the way to the beach I explained why I'd ripped the calling card to pieces. This is the lie I told. After memorising the name and address of the bar I ripped it up because there was no further use for it. In England, I stated in all seriousness, this was a normal custom.

'Really, ba why no meet me?' said Mindi.

I took the liberty of placing an arm around her shoulder.

'Because,' I replied, stressing the word, 'Karl wanted to watch the boxing tournament. After that we were going to the bar.'

Mindi didn't believe a word. 'I no care,' she said and ran away.

I gave chase. The tide was out. Little white horses danced in the moonlight, and although it was a long way away, the lovely sound of the sea was all around.

I ran and ran until the sand turned to mud. The mud was sticky and I had to take off my sandals. When I finally reached Mindi she was dancing in the moonlight. She threw her arms into the velvet night.

'Look many star!'

I gave the celestial wonders a quick glance before grabbing her.

'Wha?' she gasped with blinking eyes.

I pulled her towards me until her breasts were pinned against my chest. She resisted, protesting at my actions, but I held on tight. I placed my lips full on hers and poked my tongue out, but she wouldn't open her mouth, and after a few impotent licks I felt like a stupid dog.

Mindi pulled away until I let go at a critical moment. The momentum sent her flying into the mud where she landed with a resounding splash.

'Ewww,' she cried, with a small kitten-like yelp, 'look wha you do.'

I reached a hand down. 'Here let me help you up.'

Mindi brushed aside my helping hand and examined her mud-splattered shorts with a furrowed brow.

'Now me dirty, velly, velly dir-tee.'

Once more I moved towards her, but she held out a defiant hand, warning me to stay away. Then a mischievous glint appeared in her beady black eyes.

'Close you eye.'

'Why?'

'I wan kiss, ba no looky.'

Like an idiot I closed my eyes and pursed my lips. With a squeal of delight Mindi shoved me hard in the back, the force of which sent me headfirst into the cold slimy mud. I sat up, wiped some mud away from my mouth and eyes, and peered into the night. I was sitting on the beach in the moonlight, alone.

Mindi was nowhere to be seen. It appeared I'd made a complete fool of myself, but sometimes it's good to just act on mad impulses, and after wiping as much mud off as possible I headed back to the hotels, bars and restaurants feeling strangely groovy.

At the shore I heard the unmistakable voice of Mindi. I looked all around and saw her lying on a sun lounger. She called out my name, like she was calling out to a pet cat or something.

'Jo-Jo, come, come, Jo-Jo.'

I reached the sun lounger. Mindi pulled her legs up and clasped her arms across her knees, reminding me of a schoolgirl. I began apologising.

'I sorry too, come we dirty, we go hotel an sho-wer,' said Mindi.

In the dark I looked away and raised my eyebrows, but despite everything I didn't need a second invitation.

Next we were inside a, luxurious hotel room. A single thought flashed through my brain. Was I going to get my end away? It was anyone's guess. Mindi took charge of the situation. She produced some white towels and told me to get undressed. Apparently she was to shower first and I was to wait until she had finished and then take my shower. I agreed to her bathroom plans like a docile minion.

With Mindi inside the bathroom I threw my clothes off and wrapped a fluffy towel around me. I lay on the king-size bed and relaxed. Not before long the sound of the shower became a massive distraction. The running water encouraged me to envisage Mindi inside, naked, her wet skin glistening as she rubbed herself all over. Eventually it was too much.

I tip-toed across the room, turned the handle of the bathroom door with a deft wrist action, and slipped quietly inside. The silhouette of Mindi's naked figure was clearly visible behind a frosted glass partition. Immediately I was turned on, and Little Joe rose to the occasion, poking against the restraint of the towel. I cast off the towel and Little Joe pinged upwards, happy to be free.

I approached the bath and stepped gingerly inside. Sensing a presence Mindi turned around, saw the abomination before her, and let out an ear-piercing scream. Surprised, I slipped and landed on my arse. Mindi stared at my erect penis.

'Eeh bar ting tong, wha you do? Get out, get out,' she screamed.

I backed off. Mindi stopped shouting and stared. Unperturbed by everything, I stared right back. The water cascading over Mindi's naked body made her look like she was anointed with oil. What thighs and glorious pubic mound, and wet hair like an oil slick, and her breasts swinging to-and-fro like they were alive.

'I needed to get the mud off me, it was itchy,' I said lamely, thinking breasts a perfect creation, just like beer, a sure sign that if there was a God he knew what was going on in the world.

'Out!'

I wasn't going anywhere. I edged forward. Then Mindi did a strange thing, a thing I will always remember. She peed in the bath. The golden liquid trickled down her brown legs and into the tub.

'What d'ya do that for?' I said.

'Why, you no pee pee in bath?'

I pretended to be shocked, but watching her pee combined with all the liquid I'd consumed earlier encouraged me to follow suit. All at once I knew what needed to be done.

'No,' I announced grandly, 'I normally pee on sexy girls!' And with my cock standing to attention, a thin jet of urine shot out and hit Mindi in the midriff. For a split second she was unable to react, a frozen moment in time, but that didn't last. She started yelling and screaming more hysterically than before.

'In England we call that the golden shower,' I cried, as I leapt out of the bath and out of the room.

Sometime later Mindi reappeared with a towel tied around her head turban style, and another wrapped around her body, just above her ample bosom. I was expecting to be told to leave, but instead she sat down on the bed and leaned over.

'Come,' she said tenderly, almost motherly, 'take shower, you mud on face.'

After showering I found Mindi lying on the bed with a towel wrapped above her breasts. The towel turban was gone and her damp hair lay draped either side of her shoulders like liquorice. I lay beside her and kissed her mouth. This time she responded, her tongue darting inside my mouth with deft strokes. I felt one of her brown breasts and slipped the towel off, tracing a hand across her stomach until my fingers touched the wiry hairs of her pubes. I manoeuvred into position.

Mindi's body stiffened. She appeared suddenly vulnerable, a feeling that hinted she wasn't ready to go this far. I reached a hand down to her pussy and her big black eyes begged for sympathy.

'No entry,' she whispered.

The childlike words touched me and I stopped. Breathing an audible sigh of relief, Mindi jumped off the bed and dressed in world record time. What was she doing?

'Where ya going?'

She slipped effortlessly into her jeans.

'I go get Karl.'

My heart sank. I desperately wanted to fuck Mindi, but with Karl around it would be impossible.

'What?'

Mindi pointed at the two beds with a sweeping gesture of her hand.

'Yes Jo-Jo, Karl stay here, lot room.'

Typical of my luck. I stood up. Little Joe remained active, but I didn't give a flying fuck. He swayed from side to side as I approached, my balls swinging free and easy. I looked at my cock and then at Mindi.

'And what does eeh ba ting tong mean?' I asked imitating her high-pitched voice as I stood there in all my naked glory.

Mindi placed her hands on her hips.

'It mean crazy man in Thai!'

Then she lifted her left leg and kicked me right in the balls. It was a direct hit. I staggered backwards, dropped onto the bed, and curled into a foetal position.

Mindi opened the door.

'Yes, Jo-Jo eeh ba ting tong,' she cried, before slamming the door behind her with such force that a painting hanging on the wall fell to the floor with a resounding crash.

9.

I awoke without a hangover, a touch considering how much alcohol I'd consumed the night before. Mindi had disappeared and Karl was asleep in the adjoining bed, snoring gently, a leg twitching every so often.

An unsealed envelope lay on a bedside table. I tore it open. Inside, a note and four breakfast tokens. I glanced at my watch. It was 11.30AM. I mentally clicked my fingers. By now the breakfast service would be over and I could have done with a large fry up.

The note accompanying the letter was from Mindi and it read.

Dear crazy, nice boy. In envelop 4 token 4 breakfast. Breakfast bad, ba freee. You stay hotel 1 more night an free, no girl. Is no allowee!

Jo-Jo when you Karl back Sang Som?

If back Sang Som come me in Pee Pee family Tour I wan speak you. URGENT,

Love Min

I re-read the letter and once more for luck. So the girl loved me and the letter was proof. Understandable. Then I wondered what she wanted to speak about, it was more than a little intriguing.

As I was contemplating all this, Karl jumped out of bed like he'd been stung by a wasp. He scratched his balls, shook his head a few times, and practiced some shadow Muay Thai moves.

'What's up with you?' I said.

'Nothing wrong with me, I feel energised. I've decided to learn Muay Thai. I spoke to a guy last night and there's a place not far from Sang Som where they do lessons at a reasonable price. Anyway what happened to you, you disappeared again.'

When Karl mentioned the word boxing I remembered the bet.

'Who won the tournament?'

'The Thais won 4-1, the Danes never won another fight after you vanished. Where did you go?'

'I, I mean me and Mindi, we went to the beach.'

'Oh yes.'

'Yeah, that's when she told me about the room, and being no mug I sent her out to get you. Anyway, where's my thousand Baht?'

Karl grabbed his wallet and handed over the winnings.

'So you really like that Thai girl A?'

'Na, I would just like to fuck her.'

'Yes, I have to admit, she's a sexy girl.'

I showed Karl the letter.

'It all seems strange Joseph, I mean why this girl is prepared to help us out. Maybe she likes you, but is showing it in a Thai way?'

'Fucked if I know, anyway I've got some breakfast tokens here.'

Karl inspected the tokens.

'Excellent, I shall tell hotel staff, say we overslept and swap them for lunch tokens.'

I patted Karl on the back.

'Go to it my friend.'

Once alone I recalled the image of Mindi's naked body and it turned me on so much I was forced lie down on the bed and have a wank. As I lay there in the brief afterglow I estimated the image of Mindi in the shower would be strong enough for at least several more wanks, a comforting thought in the circumstances.

With the wank out of the way I walked into the bathroom and peered into a large mirror above a sink basin. I pulled my facial skin downwards and ran a hand through my hair.

Despite all the drink and drugs I only looked around twenty-four. That was one lucky thing my parents had passed down to me, good genes, and I still had a full head of hair, not receding anywhere, which is always a bonus for a man. In the big scheme of things I had a lot to be thankful for, even though I didn't have a career, job, money, a home, or any clue what to do with the rest of my life.

To the right of the mirror was a medicine chest. I opened it. There was no medicine inside, but plenty of soap, individual bars. I counted the bars. There were fifty-nine, all the same brand. Why were there so many? I couldn't understand it. The bars were stacked on top of each other in nine individual stacks. I wondered about those little bars of soap; in fact fixating on them. There were far too many for one hotel room and they began to oppress me, so I shut the cabinet door and banished them from my mind.

Although the bathroom was huge it was devoid of any charm, and an association of thoughts reminded me of a room I'd once rented in Indonesia. It was a cheap room, less than two dollars a night, but it possessed the world's greatest bathroom.

A flimsy bamboo door led to a small area that was cordoned off by a bamboo fence. Attached to the fence was a shower and beneath the shower was a tree stump nestled amongst a bed of large grey and white stones. By day you were showering in sunshine and by night under the stars. And if you have a 'Things to do,' list in life, showering under the moon and stars should be up there with the best.

After completing my ablutions in the bathroom with a challenging amount of soap bars, I put on my swimming trunks and headed to the hotel swimming pool. I found Karl dining in some style, seated in front of a glass table upon which several dishes of food were situated. The table was shaded from the sun by a large white parasol fringed with gold tassels, and beside the table were two wooden sun lounges. As I approached, a waiter appeared, carrying a cocktail and a bottle of mineral water on a silver platter.

'Just in time Joseph,' said Karl, 'I managed to swap the breakfast tokens for a free lunch, but had to pay for the cocktail. Do you want a cocktail?'

'I should think so amigo.'

Karl signalled to the waiter.

I had to hand it to Karl. When it came to getting something for nothing, he was the man. Moments later I was tucking into a delicious meal of chicken, black bean sauce, rice and cashew nuts.

As we digested our lunch and sipped our cocktails we discussed future travel plans. We agreed to return to Sang Som and find out what Mindi wanted. This settled the matter and I was glad Karl was coming. If he hadn't agreed to come with me I wouldn't have gone either. Sometimes life-changing events hinge on simple decisions such as these.

After the meal I jumped into the pool, swum a few half-hearted lengths, and found an inflatable ring and jumped on top. From the ring I observed the hotel and its occupants. None of the guests were speaking to each other, and aside from the aimless comings and goings of a multitude of nattily attired staff, the scene was dead.

I floated in the ring, gazed at the sky and clouds, and closed my eyes. Then I thought about the letter and Mindi and drifted off to someplace else.

10.

On our return to Sang Som town we checked into our old room above the tour operator's shop. The owners of the guesthouse welcomed us back like old friends and the shop girls' radiant expressions provided us with a perfect example of why Thailand is known as the land of smiles. Immediately we felt at home.

We ordered a couple of Chang beers and sat at a table. The girls fussed around and wanted to know all about our time spent on Pee Pee Island.

'Where's Mindi?' I asked.

'Ao Nang beach.'

Karl was restless.

'No point staying here. I'm going to hire a moped, find out about the boxing lessons. You coming?'

'Na, gonna take a walk around the town, down to the river.'

As Karl disappeared down the road and the girls became pre-occupied with a boatload of newly arrived tourists, I set off. I walked past the stall where I'd eaten my marathon dinner a few nights before. The jolly cook pointed to one of the tables, inviting me to eat with a hearty laugh.

I continued down to the river. It was late afternoon and the sky was turning several shades of purple, illuminating the town in a strange atmospheric glow. One by one, little yellow lights appeared on each of the food stalls.

In a nearby park a group of women took exercise. I listened to the shrill voice of the instructor as it echoed into the purple night, and watched the ladies jumping and stretching. A few evening joggers were out also, the sweat of their bodies glistening under bright yellow lamps that lined the riverside path like muted sentries.

It was such a peaceful scene that I grew sad and lonesome. Wherever I went in the world, I was the outsider, someone looking in at events as they transpired. How was I going to make it? I asked the river. The languid grey brown water slid by effortlessly. Here and there a long tail boat roared past and out into the distant sea beyond. On some boats the ghostly silhouettes of sailors, and here and there a red light shone romantically.

The river was at low tide and exposed an expanse of grey mudflats. The mud was reflected in the lamplight and there was movement, some small creatures swishing around in the gloom. I strained my eyes to see what they were, but it was impossible to make them out. Further along a flight of stone steps led down to the water. Having nothing better to do I decided to investigate what was slithering around down there in the mud.

I reached the steps, made my way to the last one, squatted, and peered closely. In the mud, skipping along the slimy surface with the use of front limbs, were many fish-like animals. There in front of me was evolution in action, a fish turning into a frog. I thought about evolution then, wondering if back in the mists of time one of my ancestors had indeed crawled out of the mud in search of a better life.

I leant over and managed to grab one of the fish, but in doing so fell off the step and landed flat on my stomach. I cursed and laughed out loud. I was rapidly becoming old friends with the mud of Sam Song. I looked at the fish/frog squirming like an eel in the palm of my hand. It didn't look much like me, but then I wouldn't look much like me in another hundred years, so after a few millennia who knows what might happen?

As my long lost relative blew a bubble from its thick, rubber-lipped mouth I continued to wonder. If humans really did evolve from fish where had it got us? Not far I concluded, and in reality we were still swimming around in the mire just like the mudskipper, except the mud and shit we were squirming around in was of our own making.

I lay the creature in the mud, watched as it slithered away, and made my way back to the guesthouse. It was dark by now and the purple sky had turned to one of midnight blue.

On entering the shop the three young girls held their noses.

'I fell in the river,' I said.

After showering and changing into clean clothes I went downstairs, ordered a beer, and waited for Karl to return from his boxing expedition. I was halfway through the beer when Mindi appeared, riding pillion on a moped taxi. She jumped off and ran over, wrapping her arms around me and overwhelming me all at once. She spoke very fast, a mixture of Thai and English, little or none of which I understood.

Then, before I could take another swig of beer, we were riding pillion on the back of the moped along the streets of Sang Som, Mindi's excited words tumbling into my ear, before being carried off by the wind and away into the night.

The moped turned into a dimly lit road and stopped in front of an empty building. The dilapidated structure was squashed between a Thai disco and a Scandinavian meatball restaurant. Mindi pointed at the building.

'And?' I said.

'You letter see?'

I nodded.

'This important wan ask, wan open bar, an rent only five thousand baht.'

'Sounds cheap.'

'Yah! Cheep an good loca-tion, come we eat noodle.'

I glanced at the Scandinavian restaurant. Inside, diners eating steaks and golden fries, drinking wine and beer. I halted.

'Can't we eat in there and discuss it?'

'No way, they rival.'

At the noodle stand we ordered two bowls of noodle soup and sat at a small plastic table. The soup was no substitute for steak and fries, but tasty and a tenth of the price. As we tucked into the grub Mindi gave me the low down.

She planned to open a small bar. She had everything sorted: staff, equipment, stock and all the other stuff a person needs to open a bar. The only thing she didn't have, well not enough of, was capital. This was where I came in.

She needed a business partner and all I had to stump up to be one was fifteen hundred US dollars. Fifteen hundred dollars for a twenty-five percent stake in the business. I had exactly that amount in traveller's cheques, but did I have the balls to risk the cash? There would be no written contract, just a verbal agreement and in legal terms meaningless, but it was such a small amount to invest that immediately I wanted in.

It was the chance I'd been waiting for, the chance to avoid a quick return to England and an uncertain future. I pictured myself back home: living with my parents, sleeping in my old childhood bed, my friends with partners, children, cars, houses and established careers. And there was the shit weather, unemployment queue, job hunting, giros, interviews, commuting, insane employers, soul-sapping employment, credit card debts, interest payments and spiralling overdrafts to consider. A depressing list I only had to think about it for a few moments before becoming suicidal.

Then I pictured myself as a bar owner, running things, hiring and firing, barring drunks, drinking brandy, smoking expensive cigars, and re-telling tedious anecdotes to the same bunch of regulars each and every night.

Then I thought of everything that could go wrong. Mindi could easily take my money and disappear. There were several known scams operating in Thailand, fake diamond scam, money-changing scam, boiler-room scam. I could see the headline: 'Another Farang duped in Thai confidence trick.'

There were plenty of gullible Westerners in Thailand willing to hand over cash to pretty Thai women. And yet it would take less than a month to spend $1500 travelling in Thailand. And anyway I was sick of travelling; it was rubbish, the experience overrated. The stupid tours, the stupid backpackers, the stinking cities, the same old island shit, the scuba-divers, mountain climbers, crap bars, cheap food, arduous bus journeys, annoying locals, the sheer bloody pointlessness of it all. Maybe it was time to stay put and plot up in one place for a while?

Anyway if the bar meant I got to stay in Thailand for three or four extra months it would be money well spent, anything beyond that would be a bonus. And if Mindi did run off with the money then it would be bad karma for her and I could put it down to experience.

I studied Mindi surreptitiously. She talked animatedly, eyes blazing, body language exuding sincerity. In situations like these you have to go with gut instinct. Somehow I knew she wasn't going to rip me off. This was the slice of luck I'd been praying for. This is it Ridgwell, I told myself excitedly. This is an opportunity that maybe only comes along once or twice in a lifetime. If you don't take it you will regret it for the rest of your life. Fuck it, I thought, O Sole Mio.

'It sounds like a good investment, when do you want the money?'

Mindi let out a joyous squeal.

'Tomorrow, tomorrow pay ole Chinese lady rent.'

I slipped an arm around her petite waist.

'But why do you want me to be your partner in the bar?'

'Why, why?' she stated dramatically, 'you only person help, an you my hus-ban yes?'

This outlandish declaration took me completely by surprise. Her husband, had she taken leave of her senses? Mindi brandished a large iron key in the air like a sword.

'Come, we inside bar, I have key!'

11.

The interior of the building was covered in layers of dust and a musty smell of death permeated the atmosphere. There were two floors and a rooftop, and despite being in great need of modernising, seemed a perfect location for a small bar.

Mindi gave a running commentary of where everything was going to go, laying out her vision of the bar in surprising detail. As we toured the dark and dusty premises it was obvious that this was her dream, and it confirmed my gut feeling that it wasn't a scam and she wasn't going to run off with the money.

Eventually we climbed some wooden steps that led directly onto a rooftop. We walked to the end and peered over the wall. Down below the lights of Sang Som shimmered, a cool breeze blew and stars twinkled high above. Mindi put her arms on the wall and sighed like a child, a centuries old sigh of hope.

'Yah, now help me, my dream come true, an maybe make lot money.'

The word, 'money,' filtered through to my conciseness, but was immediately dismissed. Even if the bar was a success it would never generate enough income to be worth anything to me in England, and getting my original investment back would be a minor economic miracle. Anyway, I had other matters to think about. Mindi was wearing a short skirt, which revealed a good deal of her shapely brown legs. I remembered how desperate I was to fuck her.

Without further ado I moved up close and lifted her skirt. Mindi sighed as her knickers slid down her dusky thighs, the dream of opening her own bar acting like a powerful aphrodisiac, her resistance finally broken. The moment had come.

'Yah Jo-Jo,' she murmured, 'this my dream an my dream you dream, wha you say?'

I dropped my shorts and pants.

'It's a dream come true.'

Mindi began to moan.

'Promise help me Jo-Jo?'

'Yeah, yeah.'

12.

After the rooftop encounter Mindi and I parted ways, agreeing to meet early the following day. On my return to the guesthouse I bumped into Karl wandering the dimly lit streets of Sang Som Town, like some lonely fellaheen on a forgotten journey to the end of the night. I gave him the good news about the bar, although strangely he didn't view the venture in the same positive terms.

'$1500 to be a partner in a bar, it all sounds too good to be true, and like you hardly know this crazy Thai girl,' he said.

'But think about it Karl, running a bar, not having to go home. All you gotta do is serve drinks, play some music, and let the good times roll.'

'That is not a sensible reason for wanting to go into business with anyone.'

'Listen, by tomorrow night we can be staying in the place for free.'

'I can stay rent free, no strings attached?'

'I might need a little bit of help constructing the fucker.'

Karl sighed and kicked a stone across the road.

'Shit, Okay let's do it, let's build the best bar in Thailand!'

I couldn't believe it. Karl was on my side, fighting in my corner, and the news filled me with good vibrations. Yes, with Karl backing me up surely nothing could go wrong. I held up my hand and we high-fived.

'Alright!'

13.

The next morning events moved quickly. First we witnessed Mindi's resignation. The owner of the shop, an old Thai man, was unhappy and a shouting match ensued. As angry words ricocheted around the premises, all the shop girls looked scared and Karl and I kept a low profile.

At the height of the argument, I noticed one of the girls staring at me. Something about her stare was unsettling. Her eyes implored me, maybe even pleaded with me. It seemed like a bad omen.

Eventually Mindi walked out, nose held firmly in the air.

'What was all that about?' I asked, as we made a fast exit.

'Silly old man, angree lose best sales girl an owe me money, an no wan pay, he very stin-gee!'

Dealing with the owner of the squashed house was our next move. Karl and I waited outside as the business was transacted. At one point Mindi appeared and asked for the $1500 upfront. I remembered the shop girl's unsettling stare. It made me think. Should I pull out at the last moment? No, it was impossible; I'd already stepped over the point of no return. I handed over the notes. It left me with two hundred dollars to my name, so if this pretty Siamese girl was scamming me I was well and truly fucked. Ah well, c'est la fucking vie!

Ten minutes later Mindi emerged, waving a piece of white paper Neville Chamberlain style. It was a rental contract for the property. She had paid a month's deposit and a month's rent in advance. Now all we had to do was turn the squashed house into a bar.

Inside the building the three of us discussed what needed to be done in solemn fashion, like we were creating the constitution of a new republic, rather than a tiny bar. Once everything had been decided and spoken we rolled up our sleeves, put our heads down, and got to work.

The following days passed in a blur of feverish activity. Mindi organised everything, I flapped around, and Karl proved to be industrious and indispensable. He was a painter, a carpenter, and an electrician combined, a hulking ball of energy.

Each day we started work early and continued our labours late into the evening, sweating hard and singing songs, cursing and arguing, but getting the job done. We threw stuff at each other, said crazy meaningless things, worked mad hours that nearly killed us, but within a week the bar was built, the walls painted, and the kitchen installed.

Next we recruited the bar staff. Mindi sourced three reliable local girls and paraded them before me one sweaty afternoon. Nut, Pree, and Pooh were their names and all three were young and pretty in their own way.

As the girls nervously paraded before me I made a half-arsed attempt to appear businesslike. I sat back in my chair, assumed an air of confidence, and raised my beer. I asked a few vague questions in English and the girls nodded and smiled and didn't understand a word.

Then there was the small issue of choosing a name for the bar.

'This my dream, so wan call Dream Bar,' said Mindi dreamily.

I reckoned it was a corny name, dream or no dream.

'I'm not sure about that Mindi. I know this is your dream, but we need a more memorable name, something that will stand out. Karl, what do you think?'

'Yes, for sure Dream Bar is not a good name, what about Bar of Croatia, this is good no?'

'Are you taking the piss?'

'What is wrong with this name, remember Croatia is the most beautiful country in the whole...'

I raised one arm and called for hush.

'No, no, an idea is coming to me, yes this is it...' I stopped speaking and eyeballed the others, 'The Lotus Eater's Bar!'

Karl and Mindi pulled faces.

'Ehh bah ting tong!' said Mindi

'The Lotus what?' said Karl.

46

'Think about it, it's ideal, for lotus eaters were hedonists, pleasure seekers, and daydreamers, and we can run with the theme of dreams, clouds painted on the walls, maybe even some angels or maybe we could call it Kubla Khan, or Xanadu, or The Pleasure Dome or...'

Mindi cut me short.

'Yah, no bad ideas, ba me goody name, Buddha Club after great master Lord Buddha. This Chok Dee, good luck name, an very important. For is Buddha live always Chok Dee, always luck an make lot money.'

I ran over, grabbed Mindi by the waist, and spun her around.

'That's it, that's the name, that's the name, The Buddha Club.'

'Maybe it could work,' said Karl, 'but why not bar instead of club?'

'Spot on amigo, an inspired idea, The Buddha Bar!'

Mindi yelled, screamed, and clapped her hands. 'Yah, Buddha Bar!'

So Buddha was the theme we ran with. We hired a local artist to paint a faithful representation of the holiest of holies along an entire length of one wall, and when finished, although amateurish, Buddha smiled down beatifically, giving his eternal blessing to our tiny little establishment.

We also commissioned a large neon sign of the image of Buddha to be placed above the entrance. Then we purchased a second hand hi-fi, a big old glass-fronted fridge, and all the stocks and other sundries. The last item to arrive was the neon sign, and although the rest of the building retained the appearance of a traditional Thai bar, the impressive sign gave it a hint of modernity, and caused quite a stir when it went up in the street. There it was, a huge red flaming beatific Buddha, the most revered image in all of Thailand beaming out into the immortal night.

At the end of each sweltering day the three of us sat outside our new bar drinking beer and watching the world go by. And the more we drank, the bigger we talked. If the bar was a success we would open a chain of bars, creating a brand, and selling franchises, first in Thailand and then around the world. Karl even went so far as to say he would open a Buddha Bar in Opatija. And yet we wouldn't stop there. Together we would open bars in London, Paris, New York, Moscow, and Beijing, and eventually our faces would appear on the cover of business magazines celebrating the successful, global, entrepreneurial spirit.

The night before opening I sat underneath the saintly looking Buddha mural and thought about what was happening in my life. It was definitely a strange set of circumstances, but then the last five years my life had been a perpetual strange set of circumstances. And as the gaze of Siddhartha Guatama, lord of Nirvana and the eightfold path shone out into the night, I wondered just what the immediate future had in store for me, Mindi, Karl and our funky little bar.

14.

On the morning of the grand opening, a palpable tension hung in the air, with the owners and crew visibly apprehensive. Nothing further needed to be done and so there was nothing to do, but wait around. Time passed slowly.

Around noon I walked out into electric tropical sunshine to buy a copy of the Bangkok Post. On my return I read with interest an article about the drug Ya Baa that was apparently destroying Thailand's youth and then, out of a habit invested in me since childhood, checked the English football results.

The bar remained empty all afternoon and the grand opening became a disappointing anti-climax. Yet despite the lack of custom nobody was unduly worried. All of us knew the Buddha Bar's primary function was to provide evening entertainment to the tourist trade, and subsequently we fully expected to conduct most of our business after dark.

Mindi busied herself by making banana milkshakes for everyone and we sat tight and continued to wait. Then, as we slurped our milkshakes and gazed onto the street, a middle-aged white man appeared on the scene. He didn't say hello or anything, but just stood a few feet from our premises, a concerned expression on a tired face.

Mindi leaned over.

'He owner Scandinavian restaurant, one speak you.'

I nodded and relayed the information to Karl who also nodded and proceeded to pick his fingernails with his Special Forces knife, the same one he'd used to guillotine coconuts on the porch of a tiny Malaysian beach hut another lifetime ago.

Mindi had already given us the low down on this character. He owned the Scandinavian restaurant next door, and the word on the streets of Sang Som was that he thought our small, cheaply decorated bar, was lowering the tone of the neighbourhood. It was a negative attitude that didn't bode well for any future neighbourly relations.

The dude was a pale, burnt-out man, possibly mid to late fifties, but could have been much younger, it was hard to tell. He possessed a thinning blonde thatch atop a face that had never been young. Like when you see a child that has the face of an eighty-year old. He also possessed the marble-toned skin of somebody who has been living underground for many years, and from his arms hung long, wispy, blonde hairs, a strange hirsuteness that gave him the unfortunate appearance of an albino orangutan.

'What a strange looking guy,' remarked Karl, who switched from picking his fingernails to picking his teeth with his knife.

Mindi leant against the doorway of the bar, simultaneously thoughtful and defiant.

'He thing Buddha bar no goody, he thing we po-or an shame his restaurant,' she whined.

'Fuck him,' I said.

'He stooped an silly ol man.'

'Yeah, why's that?'

'I know him. He marry loc-al girl, ting tong girl. Then come Thailan from Norways, an spen lot money on ting tong girl, buy house, car, nice cloth. She call him walking ATM man. I thing he spen all life saving. Ba although girl ting tong, she clever, when all money gone she divorce ole man an keep all everything. Then she kick ole man out an move young boyfrien an all family in!'

'How comes she got to keep everything, surely they should have split it 50-50?'

'This Thai custom, for despite marry Thai woman, Thai law say ole man alien, no legal right, no nothing him. The only thing ting tong girl left was restaurant, ba tha coz she no like do hard work all time.'

I stared at the Norwegian man, wondering why he hadn't gone home after his Thai wife stitched him up, wondering why he hadn't just packed his bags and headed back to Oslo with a tail between his legs. Maybe it was because of what the old poet once said. You can never go home.

A while later the bar girls turned up to commence their inaugural shift. They wore identical black tee-shirts; each one printed with an image of the red neon Buddha sign with the words, Buddha Bar, printed above. Collectively, they were an attractive addition to the overall aesthetic of the bar. As there was nothing for them to do I told them to sit next to us and look pretty. Then we all waited for something to happen.

And it was hot! The sun reached its apex in the sky and the heat intensified until, without moving a muscle, I began sweating cobs. In contrast not a single drop of sweat could be seen glistening on the girls. Their melanin enriched skin was built for the sun, while my fair northern European skin was built for the rain and snow.

Scandinavian tourists arrived at the unfriendly orangutan's restaurant at regular intervals, but apart from a few cursory glances they ignored our bar. It wasn't long before Mindi became agitated, the girls chattered amongst themselves, and Karl announced he was going to the beach. I walked inside the bar and grabbed another ice -cold beer. I mean what else was there to do?

Then, just as it appeared nothing was going to happen, the owners and several associates from the Thai disco appeared on the scene. Several men strolled up and walked into the bar. They were dressed in identical black suits, like the local Mafiosi.

The girls, as was the custom, adopted a deferential and sub-missive manner towards their male counterparts, as they settled down to a serious whiskey session. I sat outside the bar and watched the street. The girls were occupied attending to the re-quests of the men, which left me with nothing to do except sit out-side and try not to drink too much.

I slapped my hand down on my arm and killed my first mosquito of the evening. I peeled the squashed insect from my arm, inspected it briefly, before flicking it to the floor. Then Mindi appeared and glared at me.

'What?' I fired at her.

'Tha music.'

'What about the music?'

'We need buy modern CD, your CD ole man CD.'

I baulked at the sound of my classic recordings described thus, but Mindi was right. We needed some modern music for the modern generation. The music I had was mostly fifties, sixties and seventies product. And although I consider most modern music to be badly produced, bland and uninspiring, most young folk didn't share the same eclectic tastes. And this presented us with a problem. The nearest place to get some good quality, up to date Western sounds was in Bangkok, a city over five hundred miles away.

'I'll have to make a trip to Bangkok.'

'Yah, good idea, Bangkok goody music, mo-den.'

I thought of the trip, and all it entailed, and shuddered.

'Have we got enough money for airfare?'

'No money plane, you go coach, I free ticket, give name big shop Bangkok.'

That settled the matter.

'I'll catch the night bus tomorrow.'

An hour later about fifteen or twenty backpackers appeared on the horizon. Much to my joy I could see the long blonde hair and tall frame of Karl leading the way. Good old Karl. He hadn't just gone to the beach for a swim and to top up his tan, no, he had spoken to everyone on that beach, told them all about the bar, and managed to get a large group to come along. I had to hand it to him, he knew how to get things done and we would all miss him when he left.

'Wow, look Mr Karl, many people our bar!' cried Mindi.

'Tell the girls to get ready and get your cocktail book out.'

Moments later Karl and the backpackers poured into the bar.

'Where d'ya find all these freaks?' I said.

Karl smiled happily, happy to being doing someone a favour, just happy to be helping out.

'I met them on the beach, told them about the bar, about the music and for some reason they all want to listen to Elvis.'

'You can't fuck with the King.'

15.

Things became hectic. Eager to take advantage of the cheap cocktails the beach people issued a multitude of orders, and we were all jumping. Negotiating this chaotic scene I made it to the kitchen and poked my head around the door. Mindi was inside mixing drinks. She gestured to the icebox, the contents of which were melting rapidly.

'Need more ice,' she cried, as she simultaneously mixed ingredients for cocktails, took drink orders, and issued instructions to Nut and Pooh.

'Shall I order another box?'

Mindi shook a cocktail shaker vigorously above her head until the outside of the container frosted over.

'Ya go now, no ice we no cocktail.'

I walked through the bar, jumped onto the bar's moped, and sped off into the night. On passing the Pee Pee family shop I shouted hello to one of the girls working inside. The girl broke out into an involuntary smile, but before it was fully formed the smile vanished.

At the ice shop I communicated with the man in sign language, body language, and broken Thai/English, until he nodded his head emphatically and replied in sign language of his own, convincing me the ice would be delivered in one hour.

Job done, I mounted the moped and was just about to ride away when the girl from Pee Pee family appeared on the scene. She had one arm outstretched, indicating I wait. I cut the engine. It was the same girl who'd given me a strange look when Mindi handed in her resignation.

'Jo-Jo, speak you.' said the girl.

'What's up lady?'

The girl pointed to the other side of the road and we crossed over to a sheltered spot by the riverside.

'So what's up?' I repeated.

The girl issued a series of warnings.

'Min bad, bad, bad, care-ful!'

What the fuck?

'Why is Mindi bad, what do you mean?'

'Min bad, bad.'

'Why?'

'She danger-ous, dangerous girl whole Thai-land!'

What did this girl mean and why was she warning me off? I grabbed her by the shoulders.

'Why dangerous?'

The girl shook free from my grip and glanced over her shoulder. Standing outside the tour operator's shop, smoking a cigarette, was the owner of Pee Pee Family Tours. He wasn't best pleased to see a member of staff fraternising with a farang on his time, and he shouted something in our direction. The girl spoke rapidly in Thai before switching to English.

'I go!'

Then she ran off.

I walked to the moped in a state of shock and confusion. What the fuck was all that about? I slowed the bike outside Pee Pee family and peered inside. The girl was sat at reception, but on seeing me she pretended that she hadn't and acted like I wasn't even there.

A number of possible explanations flashed through my mind. Maybe the girl fancied me? Maybe she was jealous? Maybe Mindi was a con artist? Danger, a farang mixed up with a disreputable local girl, or maybe I'd end up in prison for working on a tourist visa? None of the explanations made any direct sense and I didn't have a clue what it all meant, but back at the bar a party was in full swing and the matter was quickly forgotten.

Karl was there, dancing with five pretty Swedish girls under the Buddha mural, holding court like Hugh Heffner.

'Croatia, you have never been there, are you mad? It is the most beautiful...' I heard him say.

Mindi took control of customer satisfaction in impressive style. She was a fund of free tourist information and flirted outrageously with all the men, which in turn encouraged them to stay longer and order more drinks. As for me, I kept a low profile so that the men might think she was available, a deliberate ploy to boost the bar's profits, and one which seemed to work.

That first night passed in a dizzy sweating whirl. After the girls left for home Karl said he was going to the beach with his new Swedish friends.

'Want to come? I think one of them might be interested.'

The girls were all pretty Nordic visions, and in any other circumstances I would've jumped at the chance, but there was still work to be done in the bar and Mindi to consider. After all I was her husband. I patted Karl on the shoulder.

'I've got business to take care of.'

'So, you're a big business man now, a?'

'Shut up, I gotta do the washing up!'

'Okay, your loss.'

'Shit, go on have a good time, but don't wake me when you get back.'

'That's if I get back.'

With Karl's departure, the bar emptied in minutes. When the last customers left I began locking up. Mindi was in the kitchen and the bar was silent, almost eerie. It was then I saw him, a Thai man, standing in the shadows some distance away. He smoked a cigarette. He flicked his cigarette into the air, causing a line of orange to appear in the night, before disappearing into the shadows.

'You wan cocktail?' asked Mindi from the kitchen.

I locked the door. The excitement of opening the bar and doing good business had left us exhilarated. We had cleared a healthy profit and everything had gone according to plan, in fact far better than either of us could have expected. I picked up a bottle of tequila and grabbed Mindi by the waist.

'Come on, let's go to the rooftop and drink to our success.'

'Wan salt an lime?'

'Bring it on.'

16.

The next morning, as we sipped pineapple milkshakes outside the bar, I gave Karl the low down.

'Karl,' I said, 'due to a lack of variety on the musical front a trip to Bangkok is now unavoidable. So-oo, seeing as how you're my best mate, I was wondering if you might oversee the bar until I return?'

'Yeah okay.'

Had I just heard what I'd heard? I was counting on at least a moan or gripe to contend with.

'I knew I could rely on you to help me out.'

'You have to do what you have to do,' he joked.

Once that was sorted I scanned the immediate vicinity until my gaze fell upon a Thai man leaning against a wall. I could have sworn I'd seen him somewhere before. He was smoking a cigarette.

'But one thing I've got to tell you Joseph and this is an important thing.'

'What's that?'

Karl slurped the rest of his milkshake down in one.

'I've already got my boxing certificate, yes?'

I nodded.

'And you remember what I said I'd do once I got it?'

Of course I remembered. How could I possibly forget? Yet, when the boxing lessons ended Karl hadn't mentioned anything about moving on, and because we all wanted him to stay for as long as possible neither had anyone else.

'Yeah I remember, once you got the certificate you said you was gonna concentrate on making the bar a success.'

'Let's be serious for a moment.'

'Okay.'

'I'm leaving Sang Som. I was going to leave tomorrow morning, but now I'll wait for you to return from Bangkok. Once you're back I will leave this place,' he said, and made a sweeping gesture with his hand in the direction of the street.

Following the direction of his hand, I caught sight of the Thai man again. When I caught his eye he smiled, a simple act that unnerved me.

'I really appreciate it Karl,' I replied hurriedly, 'you said you were gonna go and I accept that, but when you get the chance have a look at the man leaning against the wall and tell me if ya recognise him. Don't make it obvious'

Karl didn't even flinch.

'I've seen him already, and yes I've seen him before, he was standing outside the bar late last night.'

'He was?'

'Yes.'

This news immediately put me on a para.

'Maybe he's just interested in the opening of the bar,' I replied unconvincingly.

'Maybe, but he makes me uneasy.'

The fact that Karl felt uneasy was good enough to put me on a double para.

'Me too.'

Karl fingered his empty milkshake glass thoughtfully.

'It could just be coincidence, but I'm certain he has something to do with Mindi.'

This was exactly what I was thinking, a disturbing telepathy that was enough to send me into the freaky environs serious heads often allude to as the, 'triple para.'

'What makes you say that?'

'Gut feeling.'

Such a response made it imperative that the matter was clarified and the only person capable of providing such clarification was Mindi. She was doing something in the kitchen. I called out her name and motioned for her to come over. Just before she got to the doorway I looked to where the man had been standing, but the stranger was gone, disappeared into thin air.

'Wha?' said Mindi

'Er, remember I'm going to Bangkok tonight,' I said feebly.

'Ya, already ticket give you.'

'Just making sure ya remember. You can go back to what you were doing now,' I added, like I was doing her a favour.

Mindi pulled a face.

'Eeh ba ting tong,' she fired at me, before spinning around and returning to the kitchen with her nose in the air.

I turned to Karl.

'Where'd he go?'

Karl shrugged his shoulders.

'I don't know, he just vanished as if by magic.'

A wave of anxiety washed over me and freaky notions dominated the ventricles of my brain. Things were going awry and Karl noticed.

'Don't worry about it,' he said reassuringly.

But I was worried about it. It seemed something was up, maybe something sinister, but despite the freakiness of the incident I decided to change the subject.

'Where next after Sang Som?'

'Where next?' replied Karl becoming animated, 'I'm heading to the Philippines. Should be able to sign on a cruise ship at a place called Batangas, a year or two on the ship, and back home to Opatija.'

'I hope everything works out for you,' I said sincerely.

Karl wiggled his toes in his sandals.

'Thanks, but for me it is time to move on, I've started to get itchy feet again. What about you?'

I glanced at my feet. They were motionless.

17.

By late evening I was all set to catch the Bangkok Express, and as business was slack, Mindi decided to accompany me. At the station she warned me of the many dangers and distractions I might encounter in the City of Angels.

'You careful Bangkok Jo-Jo, no Pat Pong district, no girlie bar, just buy new CD, promise me?'

Promise me? This was my first visit to Bangkok. How could I not sample the seedy delights of Pat Pong, the world's most famous red light district? What was I, a mug?

'I promise.'

'Good, for this one thing I no allow.'

'Pardon?'

'It tha law.'

'What law?'

'Mindi law!'

Was she winding me up? I decided to call her bluff. 'So what happens if I break this so called Mindi law?'

A blank look came over Mindi's face. 'Have kill you,' she said in a very matter of fact manner.

'Ha, very funny Min.'

Mindi smiled a crafty-looking smile and not for the first time I wondered just who this girl really was. Then she spoke more to herself than to me.

'Yes, you jus buy CD an maybe one or two beer, an then sleeeep.'

As Mindi outlined the logistics of my trip the Bangkok Express pulled into the station. It was a yellow, red, and chrome Mercedes, an impressive sight as it rolled up to the stop with lights flashing, horn honking, dust clouds billowing in its wake.

I boarded the bus and lucked out with a window seat. Outside Mindi waved frantically and I returned her multiple waves with a royal wave, one I'd copied from Princess Margaret, the most glamorous of the Royals. Then, as Mindi blew a few kisses, I nearly died of a heart attack right there in my seat.

The enigmatic Thai man was standing right behind Mindi, smoking a cigarette and smiling his fiendish smile. I didn't know what to do, except point him out to Mindi. On glancing over her shoulder her body went rigid, before relaxing unnaturally. Then she smiled like a ventriloquist's dummy and held that false smile firmly in place.

As this strange scene was played out the bus sounded its horn and moved slowly away. The distance between Mindi and I grew bigger and bigger, but she just kept smiling. All I could do was give her the thumbs up until the unlikely couple disappeared out of sight.

Get off at the next stop was my first plan of action, but by the time the bus pulled up at the next stop it was far from Sang Som. A thousand different thoughts and possible scenarios flashed through my minds eye like scenes from a film.

Who was that man and what did he want? Was Mindi in danger? Was I in danger, or Karl, even the girls? To be honest I didn't have a clue, but after weighing up the situation I decided the man must be a former boyfriend, a worrying conclusion. At the next stop the bus was many miles from Sang Som and I decided not to overreact, play it cool, and stick to my original Bangkok plan.

As the bus continued its long journey into the sticky tropical night the events at the bus stop receded and I turned my attention to the view through the window. A red moon rose in the sky. The colour and texture of its surface fascinated me. I'd never seen it look that way before, it was a like a harvest moon, but much redder and not as large, a fire moon.

Gradually I forgot about the pyrotechnic moon and Mindi and the strange man and fell asleep. I awoke some time later to a vast metropolis spreading out forever beyond each window of the bus, Bangkok, the capital city of Thailand, the City of Angels. It was just like any other city, the same juxtaposition of wealth and poverty, huge high-rises, meandering motorways, flashing traffic, hotels, and ubiquitous advertisement hoardings.

I checked into a small rundown hostel just off the Khao San road, a favourite haunt of budget travellers. The hostel was overrun with Western freaks dressed in ethnic style clothes and souvenir beer tee shirts. I studiously avoided each and every one of them.

So there I was in Raw Rice road, famous amongst travellers and gap-year students as the starting point of all Southeast Asian adventures. The road itself was nothing to write home about, just a collection of cheap guesthouses bars, cafes, and street markets, but it was here that thousands of young travellers congregated like lemmings, eager for adventure and excitement.

I observed those young travellers and wondered about the irrepressible need for humans to converge in gangs of similar minded individuals. As for me I preferred the road less travelled or a little bit of splendid isolation. I pulled out the directions Mindi had given me. It was already late and I had to get moving.

I strode out into a hot humid city night, intent on accomplishing my musical mission. I wandered from one shopping complex to another, purchasing as much modern music I could lay my hands on, mostly party music; dance/disco compilations, greatest hits, best-ofs, and anything else that was flavour of the month in the West. There was no time to visit any of the major tourist sights, the Royal Palace, Reclining Buddha, the Venice of the East etc, but that didn't bother me because those sights had no appeal whatsoever to my traveller-jaded sensibilities.

I brought a strip of postcards from a street hawker that had all those sights, plus a few others, depicted in colour. I gave the cards a cursory glance and stuffed them in my backpack. As far as I was concerned I had now seen all the tourist delights of Bangkok.

Yet despite my apathy towards its sights Bangkok was an amazing and overwhelming city. It teemed with people and buildings and traffic and shops by the thousands, with enough shoppers to fill those shops. The tiger economy was in good shape and many Thais were living the capitalist dream of conspicuous consumption and rampant materialism. It all contributed to a heady mixture that bamboozled the senses, but by nightfall I had purchased over thirty CD's and spent all the money.

I returned to the grotty hostel with bags of shopping, sweating and tired, but satisfied that it was mission accomplished. The next bus to Sang Som left early the following morning and I was determined to catch it. This left me with one night in Bangkok. One night to experience the delights of a megalopolis improbably labelled the great city, the eternal jewel city, the impregnable city of God Indra and the grand capital of the world! I stashed my shopping under my hostel bed and went out in search of some night time entertainment, Siam style.

After a cheap meal and one large Singha beer I wandered the congested streets of Bangkok and observed the after dark scenes. The tourists, holidaymakers, travellers and gap-year students were out in force, mingled with plenty of drifters, junkies and misfits.

You saw them here and there, sitting in bars or outside cafes, Westerners who had stayed in Bangkok too long or sojourned on the road too long. I wasn't sure how they ended up like that, but wherever you travel you will find them, the lost ones who refuse to go home, the ones who can't go home.

On passing a street mirror my reflection loomed back at me. It was okay, a little wide-eyed perhaps, but I was certain I hadn't travelled too long or stayed away from home too long, but who knows? Maybe one morning, if I carried on drifting...

Towards late evening I found myself in Pat Pong, the famous red-light district of Bangkok, surrounded on all sides by neon sex shows, strip bars and a conveyor belt of prostitutes. The scantily clad girls flashed legs, tits and never-ending smiles. They cried and called out, but all I was interested in was observation. Gangs of Western men prowled the streets, old and young, the sex tourists, strange looking individuals, visages adorned with an eternal lecherous smirk. The smug attitudes filled me with disgust, and the way they walked and even the clothes they wore annoyed me.

Despite my appointment with the early morning bus, I walked into a subterranean girlie bar and ordered a beer. Inside a few listless, middle-aged and elderly Western men supped beers, each with one or two nubile Thai prostitutes at their side.

These men were clearly drinking and whoring themselves to early graves and a morgue-like atmosphere hung in the smoky air like an invisible death shroud. I located a bar stool. Within seconds a girl appeared and put an arm around my shoulder, whispering obscenities. I tried to brush her off, but she was persistent, and in a flash a hand was inside my shorts. Surprised, but wanting none of what she had to offer, I jumped up and ran away.

After that I got a taste for the beer and drank in a few more girlie bars, but they were all the same, rivers of flesh, but soulless and depressing. I paid to enter a sex show. The interior was dark and dingy and smelled like day-old sex, but I saw the ping-pong act and the smoking cigarette from the vulva trick.

Sad-looking strung-out girls approached, desperate for business, lights flashed and faces appeared and disappeared. There was nothing erotic about the performances, it was more like a freak show, and when an emaciated man made automatic love to a woman on stage, I drained my beer and left.

Outside, the streets of downtown Bangkok were empty. Rubbish littered the pavements, and nervous cats and dogs slinked around. On the way back to the hostel a transvestite prostitute approached and offered his services. I politely declined, but undeterred he made more and more outrageous offers, until in the end I was forced to leg it. That night I fell asleep dreaming of jettisoned ping-pong balls and cigarettes hanging out of vaginas and smug, smiling, Western sex tourists.

18.

The return bus journey passed without incident. On reaching the outskirts of Sang Som I was tired and hung over, but considering my Bangkok mission to be a great success, I hailed a moped taxi into town feeling upbeat.

This mood evaporated the moment the taxi dropped me outside the bar. All lights were off and there were no sign of Mindi, Karl, or any of the girls. The Thai disco was open and so was the Scandinavian restaurant.

I spotted the Norwegian Orangutan and caught his attention.

'Where is everyone?' I asked.

The orangutan smiled a sickly smile.

'Hmm English boy...'

I peered inside the bar. Everything was where it should have been with everything in its rightful place. There was no sign of a disturbance or upheaval. The only problem was that it was closed and empty when it should have been open and full.

There was nothing to do, but wait until someone showed up. I purchased a large bottle of beer from a nearby supermarket and sat at a table outside the bar. I opened the beer and supped it slowly. The image of the smiling, smoking Thai man danced before my eyes. I drank more beer, kept a vigil on the street, and exhausted all possible scenarios without hitting on any satisfactory answers.

I was well into my fourth beer when Karl showed up riding Mindi's moped, with Nut and Pooh riding pillion. Nut and Pooh looked worried while Karl strode up to the entrance to the bar without saying a word. I grabbed his shoulder.

'Why is the bar shut?'

Karl shrugged away my arm and unlocked the door in a violent manner.

'We're leaving,' he whispered.

'We're what?'

Karl pushed the door open.

'We're leaving this crazy place with these crazy people, come on get your stuff and let's get out of here!'

This was a turn up for the books. Karl seldom swore and rarely got angry about anything. It appeared I had a crisis on my hands.

'Hold on a minute, what the fuck's going on?'

Karl angrily snapped the kitchen lights on, grabbed two beers from the fridge, and handed me one.

'After you left for Bangkok two young German backpackers showed up at the bar looking for somewhere to stay. It was around three o'clock in the morning and Mindi was drunk. She flirted with these guys; you know all over them and stuff. Then she invites them to stay in the bar and I didn't like the idea?'

'She flirts with all the men, it's good for business.'

'No, this time it was different, I know she's your girlfriend, but you can't trust that woman, she's irresponsible, has no head for business, she was giving those guys free drinks...'

As Karl continued it dawned on me. I didn't really know Mindi at all. Had she opened other bars with other Westerners, a serial scammer using her undeniable charms to fleece a succession of gullible losers? And yet nothing made sense. Mindi had sunk the majority of money into the business and if the bar failed she was the only loser. Then I wondered where she got the money from in the first place and a rising panic enveloped me.

'I've got to clamp down on all that shit.'

Karl put a hand on my shoulder.

'Listen Joseph, I don't think you really understand what's going on.'

'You're right I don't, so what the fuck is going on?'

'You know the Thai man we keep seeing hanging around the bar?'

'Yeah.'

'He is Mindi's husband!'

Mindi's fucking husband? My head hurt. This shocking news blew me away and for a few seconds I was rendered speechless. I took a long swig of beer and walked around in circles in the gloomy kitchen.

'Her husband?'

'He came here.'

It was at that exact moment I realised Mindi was not around. I looked straight at Karl.

'Where is she?'

'In hospital.'

'What?'

'Mindi was upstairs with the German boys and he got in.'

What the fuck was Mindi doing in the same room as the Germans?

'Why is she in the hospital Karl?'

'Her husband managed to break into the bar while we were asleep. He found Mindi and the two German travellers sleeping in the same bed and went schizo.'

'Jesus Christ.'

'That's when I heard the screams and ran downstairs. It was a strange feeling, there was hardly a sound, but blood was everywhere and I saw her.'

'You saw her?'

Karl pointed to the middle of the floor.

'She was lying over there, I thought she was dead. He stabbed her several times, she could hardly speak. With all that blood, it didn't look good. I flagged a taxi and rushed her to the nearest hospital. She's in there now, under observation.'

'She's alive?'

'Yes she's alive, lost a lot of blood, but the cuts were only superficial.'

'Right where's the hospital, I have to see her.'

'Fuck that,' hissed Karl angrily, 'she's mad and the whole situation is crazy. You wise up and come with me to Batangas.'

'I still got to see her.'

'Are you crazy? Didn't you just hear what I said? Her husband sliced her up, what if you are next in line?'

Karl was right. The sensible decision was to light out of Sang Som at the first available opportunity, but my whole life had long ago stopped making any sense, and I had to see Mindi even if it was only to say goodbye.

'I still gotta see her, will you ride me there?'

Karl threw the keys to the moped at me.

66

'I think you ride yourself.'

I caught the keys mid-air.

'But I don't know the way.'

'Take one of the girls, they'll show you. I will look after the bar until you return. Then I'm out of here.'

The situation was fast becoming untenable, but I was angry. Who did he think he was? So what if the guy was Mindi's husband? He had no right to stab her, or anyone for that matter.

'Cheers Karl, I should do what you say, but I need to speak to Mindi.'

Karl looked at me strangely and said a disturbing thing.

'Okay, it's your funeral.'

Outside, I found the girls huddled around a table, looking scared. I jumped on the moped.

'Who wants to show me the way to the hospital?'

The girls exchanged whispered words and held their heads down.

'Nut?' Nut didn't look up. 'Pooh?' Pooh didn't look up.

In desperation I turned to Karl. I held out my hands in a gesture of helplessness. Karl stepped out shaking his head.

'I don't blame them,' he muttered, as he jumped onto the back of the moped.

Just as I was going to kick start the engine an important detail needed clarification. I turned to Karl.

'Where are the two German pricks?'

'You don't have to worry about them. They caught the first bus out of town and, believe me, after what they experienced they will not be returning to Sang Som in a hurry.'

19.

I parked the moped outside the entrance of a small public Thai hospital. Karl lit a cigarette and took a drag.

'Don't be long, this place gives me the creeps.'

'If I'm longer than 30 minutes, you can go.'

Karl gave the hospital a disapproving look.

'Call it a hospital, more like a chicken shed.'

It was a standard Thai public hospital and, despite the primitive accommodation, was clean and well organised. After announcing my presence at reception I was given a note and led into a great hall. Row upon row of blue curtains lined both sides of the vast room. The curtains segmented a series of kennel-sized rooms, and along one length stood a line of Thai women. The women wore identical tent-like dresses and all were in advanced stages of pregnancy.

As I approached the nurses' station the tepee-wearing women turned their heads at the same time and stared at me. It was a remarkable feat of synchronisation and, in the state I was in, an unnerving sight. Being the only non-Asian and male I was evidently a curiosity.

Unperturbed, I marched over and handed a note to one of two nurses manning the station. The nurse read the note and shook her head. She handed the note to the other nurse. The second nurse read the note and shook her head and looked to the first nurse with a quizzical expression. I shuffled my feet and glanced towards the ceiling. I was getting pissed off. The first nurse took back the note and started to re-read it.

This charade went on a while until I pulled out a wad of Baht and peeled off a five hundred note. The nurse smiled radiantly and took the note. Then, like magic, a wave of recognition appeared on her face and she led me to a kennel in a far corner of the room.

The corrupt health worker swished aside the blue curtain and there was Mindi, lying asleep on a small camp bed, ashen faced. I indicated to the nurse that I wanted to be left alone, and re -drew the curtain. Mindi's long black hair lay to one side of her head like a miniature oil spill, her large eyes were closed, and two white spots of saliva had emerged from each corner of her voluptuous mouth. I studied her face. Her skin was pale and sickly and for the first time I saw how Thai she was.

She was a descendent of the Akha people, ancient rice growers from China, Laos, Burma and Thailand. Her cheekbones were high and prominent, her nose wide. Although identical as human beings, culturally we were a million miles apart. What was I doing there? What had I got myself into? It could never work between us and I was acting the fool, a madman, intent on just enjoying myself and never taking life seriously.

I pulled a cigarette from a pocket and placed it in my mouth. The cigarette stuck to my lip, hanging there precariously. I gave one of Mindi's feet an affectionate squeeze. It failed to wake her. This spooked me because she was very grey, and for a moment I feared she might be dead. An inappropriate thought inserted its malignant self into my brain. If she was dead would I have to pay for her funeral? I leaned over to check her breathing, but before I got close enough the dangling cigarette fell from my lip and landed in her left eye.

Mindi sat bolt upright in bed, eyes open, like a trapped and frightened animal. The offending cigarette fell off the bed and rolled across the tiled floor.

'Jo-Jo, you come,' she cried weakly.

I examined her wounds, slashes across neck, arm, both thighs and a deep gash just above her right breast.

'He try cut off,' said Mindi, caressing her ample bosom and shooting it a concerned glance.

I studied Mindi. Despite everything it appeared she was going to be okay, she was going to live. I paced the room. It was time to start getting to the bottom of this mess.

'Why didn't you tell me about this husband business?'

'No my hus-ban, ex-hus-ban,' sobbed Mindi.

'And that makes it all right!'

'No, no hus-ban hear our bar, thing lose face, an come get money. No money an angree, wan kill me!'

'But why should you have to give him money?'

'Him lose face, important thing Thai people.'

'And what about German people, was it an important night for them?'

Mindi caught her breath and smiled in a weird crafty kind of way. 'Ya, me good, ba two Germ boy jus friend. Bad luck husban see them, for lose more face lot then.'

This made more sense than the financial aspect.

'So it was more than just losing face, it was also to do with catching you in bed with two men.'

'Jo-Jo, no angree, jus boy, nothing happen, believe me?'

'You expect me to believe that?'

'Yah.'

Did I believe her? I wasn't sure, maybe it was all an act and I was a mug. Doubts entered my mind, each new doubt demolishing the old doubt, until I didn't know what to believe. I tried catching Mindi's eye, but she skilfully avoided eye contact, and came up with one heartfelt excuse after another. Gradually I began to sympathise. After all she was the victim in the whole crazy affair. I mean, she could've got killed.

'How you here?' asked Mindi.

I remembered Karl and looked at my watch. The thirty minutes had long since past.

'Shit, I came with Karl, but he isn't going to hang around.'

'Wha, who run bar?'

'The girls, why?'

'Wha, oh nooo, we go, go, pay hospital an back there!'

I held out my hand in classic halt mode.

'You're not going anywhere lady; you might have punctured a lung or something.'

'My lung fine!'

There was no doubt about it, Mindi's lungs sounded in perfect working order.

'Okay let's go.'

Funnily enough Mindi was less concerned about her injuries and well-being than the fact that the girls had been left in charge of the bar.

'Those girls pretty, but very stoo-ped,' she explained, as we checked out of the hospital.

Outside Karl was still leaning on the moped, smoking a cigarette, but as soon as he saw Mindi the cigarette dropped from his mouth.

'Don't ask,' I said.

All three of us jumped on the moped and Karl kick started the engine.

'You definitely have balls Mindi,' he shouted.

'Yah I ball, more ball tha men!'

20.

We arrived at the bar to discover that, in our absence, a group of male travellers had hijacked the place and a party was in full swing. Nut and Pree were sprawled across the laps of two young men, downing shots of tequila, and playing a drinking game. One of the guys had his hand on Nut's thigh, and her arms were wrapped tight around his neck. On the table was a half-empty bottle of Jose Cuervo. Surrounded by five young men, Pooh was holding an ice-bucket and laughing and joking. The bucket was full of red bull, vodka and straws. Another two guys were standing behind the DJ area, messing around with my new CD's, while two more were helping themselves to drinks behind the bar. Of course this state of affairs could not possibly be allowed to continue.

When Mindi clocked the scene, despite her fragile state, she dragged the girls into the kitchen and berated them in rapid high-pitched machine-gun Thai. Meanwhile, me and Karl strode in and eyeballed the free loaders.

'Hey man, come on in and join us,' slurred one of the shot drinkers.

'Join you in what?' said Karl.

The traveller hiccupped and waved his arm in the general vicinity.

'Well, can't you see man, the captain's out to lunch and the, hic, sailors have taken over the ship.'

Karl turned to me.

'Shall I chuck him out?'

Without a word I locked the door, switched the music off, and ordered the whole group to line up under the Buddha mural. Karl stood in front of them, arms folded across his chest.

'One false move and you are all so much toast,' he barked ferociously.

The young travellers were now frightened and confused.

'What the fuck's going on?' asked the shot drinker.

'Shut the fuck up,' said Karl.

I walked into the kitchen. Mindi was shouting at Pooh and Nut, but was even paler than before and green around the gills.

Then, in the middle of an especially long rant, she collapsed. I reacted just in time, but the weight of her body caused me to slip and crumple to the ground.

'Quick, help me,' I cried.

The girls rushed over.

'Mister Jo-Jo, you okay?' asked a worried looking Pooh.

In the circumstances, it was somewhat unbelievable that Pooh appeared more worried about me than Mindi, but funnily enough I was okay.

'Come on, help me get her upstairs.'

'Yes, we do.'

The four of us carried Mindi to the bedroom. We lay her down in bed and tried to make her as comfortable as possible. I told the girls to look after her and see that she got some rest, and rushed off to confront the freeloaders.

Once downstairs I explained the situation to a bunch of drunken and bewildered travellers in a clear and concise manner, asking politely that they pay for the drinks and telling them, in no uncertain terms, to get the hell out of my bar.

Surprisingly the travellers became vociferously belligerent, arguing that the girls told them it was okay to get their own drinks. This was probably true. Then they told me that they had planned to settle the bill when they left, which probably wasn't true. The only problem was that they couldn't remember how many drinks they had consumed.

'You'll have to do better than that guys,' I said.

'Yeah,' growled Karl.

After much bickering and several offers, most of which I turned down straight, the travellers eventually came up with an acceptable amount. Then, to show there were no hard feelings, I gave them a couple of vodka and red ball ice buckets on the house. With that the freaks went crazy calling me and Karl the coolest guys on the planet, and that we rocked and were awesome and other lame, youthful, exuberant, drunken shit.

Once that matter was settled I rushed back upstairs to check on Mindi. I found the girls lying on the bed like three little children. Pooh and Pree were playing with Mindi's hair, while Nut looked on with an expression filled with concern and wonderment. I told the girls to go downstairs and help Karl and after further fussing over Mindi, they smiled and left the room.

I lay beside Mindi.

'How are you?' I whispered.

'I fine, Jo-Jo, you no leave me?'

The vicious attack by her husband made me more determined than ever to stay on a little longer. 'No, but you have to promise me one thing?'

'Wha?'

'Don't keep any secrets from me ever again.'

'No Jo-Jo, you everything me.'

'Good, because from now on it's just me and you, Karl is leaving tonight.'

'He leave us?'

'Yeah, he has to return home. Make sure you get plenty of rest, I'll see Karl off at the bus station.'

'I go you, see Karl...' whispered Mindi, but before the sentence was complete her eyes closed and she fell into a deep exhausted sleep.

Downstairs everything was running smoothly. More customers had arrived and the girls were busy serving drinks. Karl was talking to three girls and the freeloaders were dancing and grooving out to the music.

After all the events of the day I was suddenly thirsty. I grabbed an ice-cold beer from the fridge, popped the cap, and drank half the contents down in one gulp. Immediately I felt better. I counted the takings and hid the money in the usual place, inside a wooden Buddha that sat on a shelf in front of a poster of the Thai King and Queen.

After finishing the beer I fixed myself a large gin and tonic, supped it slowly, and observed the scene. One of the free-loading shot-drinkers approached the bar.

'Say Mr Buddha Bar owner, where can we get some of that Ya Baa shit I've heard everyone's on in Thailand.'

Ya Baa was a highly addictive and potent concentration of methamphetamine, a popular recreational drug in Thailand and elsewhere in South-east Asia. I looked at the kid. He was young, innocent looking, untouched and untested by life, but if I didn't tell him someone else would.

'You'll get some in the disco next door, but be cautious, the penalties for possession are outrageous.'

'Thanks Mr Buddha Bar, that Ya Baa, it means crazy drug doesn't it?'

For some reason I didn't like the way the kid spoke to me. I lunged forward and grabbed him by the throat.

'Yeah, and you'd be crazy to take it, but that's up to you, but remember one thing,' I hissed into his face, 'you didn't have this conversation with me, okay?'

Shot kids eyes bulged out.

'Yeah of course, no worries man!'

Once I'd laid down the law I decided to be more sociable and, after releasing his neck, offered the kid a B52 cocktail. The kid rubbed his neck.

'Do I have to pay?'

I fixed two B52's and lit the drinks with my lighter. 'On the house amigo.'

'Hey, cheers man.'

I handed a glass to the kid. 'Drink up,' I said.

We downed the shots.

'Where ya from kid?'

'BC, I mean British Colombia.'

The kid looked around eighteen or nineteen and was bound to have a couple of worried parents, back there somewhere in the west of Canada.

'Listen, be careful if you do take Ya Baa,' I warned, 'the strength varies from one pill to the next. There's no quality control. The majority are made in makeshift factories on the other side of the Burmese border, so promise me you'll only take a half at a time and no more than one.'

Shot kid shook his head and solemnly promised to never take more than one so long as he lived and breathed. Then he ran back to his mates to tell them the good news and forget all about the warning. I grabbed a beer, changed the CD and put on 'You

Really Got Me' by The Kinks. As soon as the classic guitar riff sounded the bar went mad. Whatever way you look at it old time music is often the best. So for the next hour I played a succession of oldies and the bar was jumping.

Then, around midnight, the girls began hovering around the DJ area. At first it didn't register as to why they were there, but they looked at me in such a strange way that I was forced to ask the question.

'What's up ladies?'

At first none of them said anything. Then Pooh gave Nut a nudge.

'We leave now Mister Jo-Jo.'

'Okay, see ya tomorrow.'

The girls exchanged nervous glances.

'No, we leave now,' repeated Nut.

It was then that the penny dropped; it was pay time. I raided the wooden Buddha and gave each of the girls an extra day's wages. Mindi wouldn't have done the same, but under exceptional circumstances I figured it was only fair to give the girls a bonus.

Not long afterwards all of our customers headed to the Thai Disco. Karl helped collect glasses and empty ashtrays and I switched the lights off and locked the door. It was closing time at last.

I was now tired and felt like listening to something mellow. I put on a Stan Getz CD, grabbed two beers, and sat down under the Buddha mural. As I handed Karl a cold beer the melancholy saxophone of 'Insensatez,' echoed around the walls.

'You still leaving?'

Karl took a large swig of beer and replied without answering my question.

'Are you going to be okay here after what happened?'

'I'll be all right, you know me.'

'Yes, that's the problem, I do know you.'

'Ah, shut up, come on let's make a toast.'

Karl clinked his bottle against mine.

'Do you think her husband will return?'

'No, I don't think he will.'

'Neither do I.'

In times like these you need a friend and the words Karl said were exactly the words I wanted to hear. His answer reassured me and there are times when everyone needs reassuring.

We sat and drank in silence for a few moments.

'I've missed the night bus,' said Karl.

'You have?'

'I have.'

'Only one thing to do then.'

'And what's that?'

'Have a last big night together!'

21.

In the Thai disco a high speed techno with a thumping baseline and manic drumbeat pounded from the speakers, and the crowd performed various moves of a popular dance that can only be described as a cross between the stomp and the pogo.

We came across the freeloaders on the dance floor. They had obviously scored some Ya Baa, and were stomping away to the hypnotic music. There was shot kid, naked from the waist up, a tee shirt tied around his head like a makeshift bandanna.

I tapped him on the shoulder. 'What are the pills like man?'

'Ya baaaaaaa! Man yeah, fucking yeah, ooh, ooh, arghhhhh...'

After that incomprehensible encounter Karl and I retreated to a balcony and observed the scene.

'Hold out your hand,' Karl said.

'Why?'

'Just do it man!'

He dropped a small white pill into my open palm. I glanced at it lying there and quickly closed my fist.

'Is that what I think it is?'

'Ya Baa, you know the crazy drug. I thought we might try it out before I leave the country, I've already taken mine.'

I opened my palm and stared at the little white pill with curious eyes. Speed was in no way my drug of choice. It was mostly a functional drug: the drug of prostitutes, shift-workers and long-distance lorry drivers. And from experience it ruined your insides, like rot the stomach or something. Nevertheless I chucked the pill down my throat.

The next couple of hours flew by in a whirl of dancing and drinking. Karl scored some more Ya Baa and we necked another two pills each. Then we were talking to anyone and anything. Around three a.m. people began exiting the disco in droves and we found ourselves outside the joint, wondering what to do next. Karl was sweating profusely, his pupils so dilated you could no longer tell his eyes were blue.

'What we going to now?' he panted, as locals jumped on mopeds and rode off into the remains of the humid night.

'Meatball stall,' I said, between grinding teeth.

Karl's usually impeccable English began to disintegrate.

'I don't much appetite, my stomach has it shrunk? Why you is hungry?'

Come to think of it, I had zero appetite. I glanced towards the bar. I wasn't ready for sleep, but at least we could sit inside and talk shit for the next four or five, or however many hours it required us to come down. I pointed at the bar, but was unable to speak properly.

'Bar, let's dream, shit,' I mumbled, and burst out laughing. Karl eyeballed me strangely.

'What laughing for?'

'I sound just like that freeloading shot kid.'

'What?'

'Let's get some beers.'

Once inside the bar I grabbed two beers from the fridge, while Karl practised his recently acquired boxing moves in front of me. I handed him a bottle.

'Naa fuck drinking, it'll only bringing me down, me have coke,' he said, as a foot shot out just past my left ear. He spun around until a foot stopped just inches from my nose. I stepped back a couple of paces just to be on the safe side.

'Up to you,' I said, and passed him a coke from the fridge.

Karl downed the coke in one long guzzle.

'Put music on man,' he said and burped loudly, 'shit ya, this stuff really sticking to his teeth.'

I went to the sound system and picked out a New York Dolls CD and was just about to blast out 'Trash', when I remembered Mindi.

'Mindi,' I hissed.

Karl stopped practising his moves.

'Fucking oh no, yeah I forgetting.'

'We'll have to go somewhere else.'

'Let go a walking the town.'

'Yeah good idea, but we'd better check on her first. To see if she needs anything.'

We crept up the stairs as quietly as possible, but every creak and rustle sounded like it was multiplied a million times. Karl began laughing. I began laughing. Soon we were in hysterics. I shushed Karl and he shushed me. It wasn't that we found the situation funny, we just couldn't help ourselves.

I held a finger to my mouth and poked the bedroom door open with an outstretched foot. Inside, the room was dark and Mindi was fast asleep, grey looking, corpse in the casket style. We turned to each other and gave the thumbs up sign.

Without another thought or damned care in the world we left the bar and walked out into a fast disappearing Sang Som night. It remained humid, but a cool breeze was blowing. We kept walking. It was the best way, keep walking and don't worry where you might end up. Our energy levels, boosted by the Ya Baa circulating in our bloodstreams, remained at optimum levels. It was late by now, the town desolate, bars and shops closed. Occasionally we heard the distant drone of a moped echoing languidly into the atmosphere.

Karl broke out into a jog and urged me to do the same, and we ran into the night, towards the inexorable start of another day. With the Ya Baa in our systems we felt powerful, like we could run a marathon, or run forever, or even live forever. In that moment we were a cool breeze that nobody would ever catch, always one step ahead of the others, one step ahead of the game, a game that would surely drag us down one day, but that day seemed a long, long, way away, as far as a brilliant sun on a never-ending horizon.

Eventually we came to the riverside and stood beneath a street lamp, which illuminated the darkness in a hazy, circle of yellow light. Karl stared long and hard at the river.

'Life strange you think?' he said.

I noticed all the many eddies and swirls of the river, and wondered what it was all about and why were we there, but no answers were forthcoming. The river just rolled on by.

'Stranger than the strangest.'

Karl continued staring at the river. A blank look came over his face. I became fearful. Was he going to ask or tell me something I didn't want to hear? Reveal some personal tragedy? I hoped not. Then, just as suddenly, his demeanour changed. He smiled and clapped his hands.

'Come we for sure going meatball place I hungry now.'

Yet, by the time we got there, the meatball stand had long since closed. It was past four o'clock by this time and apart from a cat that strayed across a road with its tail in the air, the streets were deserted.

'Let's go beach,' said Karl.

'Excellent idea, but we'd better stock up on some booze first.'

On our return to the bar I took enough beers to fill the basket of Mindi's moped and grabbed a bottle of tequila. Then I thought about Mindi and her near-death experience, lying upstairs, recovering from her knife wounds. What if she needed help or assistance during my absence? What if she suffered some sort of setback? The decent thing to do was stay and look after her. Karl saw me hesitate and read my mind.

'She okay, an sure we be back before she waken.'

'Come to think of it she has taken a lot of sedatives, she'll be out for hours,' I said, but as I locked the door pangs of guilt rippled my mind.

Still, it felt good to leave all of our troubles far behind, liberating. Space, that's what I needed, space from everything, from Mindi, the bar, the girls, violent ex-husbands, idiotic tourists, even Sang Som town. SPACE.

We rode along small country roads, flanked either side by impenetrable jungle. I swigged from a bottle of beer and felt the luxury of wind in my hair. Karl drove fast and focused, concentrating fully on getting us to the beach.

I stared at flashing jungle scenes on either side of the road. Images blurred and reality distorted. I began hallucinating. The jungle appeared to be moving. The trees and bushes transformed into weirdie creatures and gruesome phantoms. Marvelling at the crazed visuals a wave of anxiety gripped me. Was it possible I was going insane?

Then, just when I'd gotten the hallucinations under some sort of control, I spotted a giant snake by the roadside. It was the biggest snake I'd ever seen, almost as big as a tree trunk, an unbelievable sight.

'Did you see the size of that fucking snake?' I shouted above the roar of the engine.

Karl shook his head.

I looked behind. The snake was still there. 'Go back, go back, it's fucking massive!'

Karl turned the moped around in a wide curve.

'Where it?'

I pointed to the side of the road. Karl zoned in, but just before we got to the gargantuan reptile I did a double take. Mother, what I thought was a snake as big as a tree trunk was, in fact, a tree trunk! Karl hit the brakes and the moped skidded to a halt.

'Is you snake?' he asked with a crooked smile.

The whole scene freaked me. I looked at the tree trunk and then at the bottle of beer in my hand. After downing the dregs I chucked the bottle into the jungle.

'Shit I'm hallucinating, pass me the tequila, I need something stronger than beer.'

Karl opened the tequila, took a hit, and handed it to me.

'Yes, need too, seeing much weird shit and, but didn't anything I no say.'

The fact that Karl was tripping put me at ease. It meant we were in the same boat, the same psychedelic mystery bus of universal nothingness. Fuck it, I wasn't totally losing the plot and nor was he. I took an extended swig from the tequila bottle.

'Don't worry, it's got to wear off if we keep drinking!'

We rode without stopping, until the jungle fell away to reveal a row of shops and bars. In front of the parade of shops was a wide expanse of beach, hemmed in by towering limestone cliffs. We drove down a tiny dirt track and parked the moped on the sand. The beach was deserted and the sea was dark. On the horizon the night rapidly faded to grey.

I discarded my sandals and walked across the cool sand. The water was dead calm, as if it was sleeping, and about five hundred metres from land a small wooden boat bobbed on the horizon. Karl was beside me and an amazing telepathic coincidence occurred.

'Let's have a contest to see who can swim to the boat first?' we said, in unison.

Without hesitating we stripped down to our pants, but just as Karl was about to run into the sea I called a halt to proceedings. As Karl was fitter than me I figured I needed a head start.

'Let's start from over there,' I said, pointing to nothing in particular.

'Over where?'

I hit the water running and swam forward with powerful strokes. From somewhere the sound of Karl's protestations echoed into the atmosphere. Having cheated I wanted to make sure I got to the boat first, but with victory in sight, something grabbed my leg and pulled me under. When I resurfaced Karl was ahead, swimming furiously.

Karl made it to the boat first, but only by an arms length and we climbed in together and collapsed onto a wooden bench. The sun was now rising in the East, an elegant swathe of pink on the distant horizon. Exhausted, we sat hunched on the bench, unable to speak.

It was probably the combination of drink and drugs that made Karl open up, but once started he didn't stop. He rambled, mentioning stuff about the folks back home, friends of his and people he had grown up with. I listened and yet I didn't listen. My own mind meandered. I thought of the past, the present, and the future. I remembered old friends, family, my old life. I remembered the years spent in Australia, in Sydney and Kings Cross and the big trip to Mexico. Had any of that ever happened? Who was I, where was I, where was anything? I closed my eyes and a million digital images exploded behind my eyelids.

'You hear me Joe?' said Karl.

I opened my eyes. 'What?'

'You hear me?'

'I hear ya.'

'I say, what think you, boat, flying in space, universe, just me and you and this small, small boat.'

High above a lone sea eagle floated effortlessly on invisible thermal currents. The sky was blue now and a big yellow sun climbed steadily upwards. Then it hit me. The boat was the answer to life's mysteries. Life was just a boat floating in the sea, going nowhere and doing nothing. It just floated. And that's what we were doing; floating through time and space, in a dream limbo.

'I think you could be right. This boat is the boat of life, a dharma, a mantra, a scripture of the golden eternity, Buddha's golden boat of eternity.'

Karl smiled a goofy, lopsided grin.

'Yeah, but glad this Buddha boat. It like a therapy, therapeutic, come we swim back.'

On the return leg we didn't race but took our time and floated in the sea, remarking on how beautiful it was in the early morning sunshine, everything tinged with a soft yellow light. The scene contained an aura of magic, an aura of saintly spiritual wisdom of ages. Unreal. At the beach we had a couple more hits of tequila and lay down on the sand. I could feel the last remnants of artificial energy departing and closed my eyes. The effects of the Ya Baa had finally worn off, and I was pleased and it felt good. I fell into a deep and exhausted slumber.

22.

I awoke to screams and voices all around. Beside me was the bottle of tequila, lying on its side, empty. I wiped some sand from my face. Many people were sunbathing on the beach, the sun was high in the sky. Another ear-piercing scream forced me to look in the direction of the commotion. What the fuck? There was Karl staggering along the beach, holding a big fat woman in a bear hug. Another fat lady was running alongside, shouting and hitting him over the head with a plastic water bottle.

I picked up the tequila and drained the last couple of drops. What was Karl doing? He appeared to be trying to throw the fat lady into the sea. Despite being physically strong, the woman's gargantuan frame was too much, and he floundered in the sand. He swayed from side to side, his left leg buckled, and they crumpled to the ground in an undignified mess. I tossed the tequila bottle aside and dashed over. Karl lay there grinning, while the woman flapped beneath him like a beached whale. Her friend shouted at me in German or Dutch or some other European shit. She was angry.

Karl opened his eyes, recognised me briefly, before closing them again.

'Let's get the fuck out of here!' I yelled.

'Ya baaaaaa,' roared Karl.

I kicked him in the gut and slapped his face. He roared once more, but didn't budge. I looked around. The women screamed hysterically. Nearby was a small boy building a sandcastle with bucket and spade. I rushed over and nicked the kids bucket and filled it with seawater. I chucked the briny contents over Karl's comatose head. He roared with indignation, but the shock made him jump to his feet.

As we ran off down the beach I took a quick look behind. The fat woman was on all fours and pointing in our direction. Standing next to her was the little boy and father. The father shook an angry fist. The fat woman's friend was with two Thai policemen. One of the policemen pulled out a gun. I pushed Karl.

'Quick, no time to lose, back to the moped now!'

Karl rubbed his head, squinted his eyes, and smiled like a big dope.

'Come on, move it,' I ordered.

Somehow the scene had morphed from a great night's adventure into a dangerous, liberty threatening situation. I screamed at Karl to hand me the keys to the scooter, but he just looked at me in blank confusion. I raided his pockets until finally, like a small miracle, I located the fuckers. We jumped on the bike and I lucked out and kick started the engine first time.

'Right, don't let go and don't fall off,' I yelled, before driving away from the beach without once looking back.

23.

We arrived in Sang Som town; tired, wasted and I, for one, riddled with guilt. In the cold hard light of early morn it was obvious I'd deserted Mindi in her hour of need, a selfish and irresponsible move. And yet it needed to be done to maintain my personal sanity in the midst of a crazy situation. The girls were sitting outside the bar talking and gossiping including, surprisingly, Mindi. She still had her bandages on, but looked completely recovered, even radiant. When the girls saw us they gasped and expressed shock, all except Mindi who sat there stony-faced, arms folded across her ample bosom.

'Where go?' she demanded, as we staggered inside the bar, 'thing hus-ban kill you!'

Realising the full extent of my selfish behaviour I decided the best tactic was to make light of the incident.

'Don't be silly, we only went to the beach, it was Karl's last night.'

Karl collapsed onto the cushions, underneath the Buddha mural, mumbling something about catching the next bus to Bangkok. My friend's dishevelled appearance immediately diffused the situation.

'I thing no Bangkok, Karl look how say, like shit.' said Mindi.

I agreed. 'Yeah amigo, you'd better stay another night and recuperate.'

Karl opened his eyes.

'What time next bus to Bangkok, Min?'

'Bus leave soon, less thirty mins.'

'I go on that bus.'

Despite protestations that he should stay another night, Karl was true to his word, and after hurriedly packing his things he bid us a final farewell. There were kisses and tears and hugs all round. Then, after promising to stay in touch a hundred times and inviting everyone to visit him in Opatija, it was agreed I should accompany my friend to the bus station.

At the station Karl just had time to purchase a one-way ticket before it was time for the last goodbye. I was in pieces, emotionally fragile and physically weak, finding it difficult to stay awake. Karl looked mashed, eyes bloodshot, face pale.

'You'll probably sleep all the way,' I said.

Karl smiled weakly.

'For sure, I will.'

'Go on, I hate goodbyes, get on the bus and get out of here.'

Without another word Karl turned around and walked towards the bus. Then he stopped halfway, pulled something out of his backpack, and walked back to me.

'Here, this is yours,' he said, and shoved his prized Special Forces knife into my hands.

I looked at the object I had always coveted, but there was no way I could take it. An overwhelming urge to start crying took a sudden hold of me and I fought hard to control my raging emotion. Karl was really a good friend and in a short space of time I'd grown closer to him than friends I'd known all my life. But maybe that is the nature of friendships; they have a use-by date, like a tin of beans or a car tyre.

'No Karl I can't....' The Bangkok bus was moving away. I ran alongside the bus and peered into windows, but only the faces of strangers peered back, and Karl was gone.

24.

After Karl's departure I settled comfortably into bar life in Sang Som town, but for weeks afterwards I kept my eyes peeled for the sinister, smiling face of Mindi's ex, especially when walking the streets alone. As an added precaution I slept with Karl's Special Forces knife tucked safely under my pillow, just in case the smiling assassin decided on a return visit in the dead of night.

Mindi's wounds healed quickly and, although scarred for life, she was relieved that the incident had occurred. For, as she repeatedly told me:

'Now got face no trouble me more an me okay, just small scar, when maybe do different, I die!'

I figured it was a Thai thing.

Almost imperceptibly the hot, humid, dusty weeks merged into one and time melted away. Due to a lack of custom we abandoned lunchtime opening. I put the lack of trade down to the harsh tropical daylight. In that unforgiving light the little bar looked cheap and uninviting while in the night-time, with Buddha lit up in red neon, it was a far more attractive proposition.

At first I thought the shorter opening hours would enable me to spend more time at the beach, working on my tan, writing poetry, and watching the girls go by, but this proved unrealistic. Although the hours were shorter, the nights were long, and on more than a few occasions we shut just as the sun rose in the East. It was a rare day if I ever got out of bed before noon and more often than not I didn't get out of bed until mid afternoon, especially if I'd consumed too much alcohol the night before.

In the tropics the only time worth doing anything is either early morning or sundown. In between it's too hot and too bright. When the sun shines at its full magnitude the colours emanating from the surrounding environment make it hard to focus. Things can deceptive: objects, horizons, vistas, even people. You had to be careful. Viewed from distance a small shiny object in the road could take on the proportions of an explosion.

Despite our best efforts the fickle nature of the tourist industry made it a struggle to turn a profit. We experienced one busy night followed by four quiet nights, one busy week followed by two quiet ones. We were never able to get ahead, and although we weren't losing money we weren't making any either, an extremely demotivating factor.

Also, running a bar was not all it was cracked up to be. The reality was nothing like the dream. It became like any other job: monotonous, tiring, and although there were no insane bosses telling us what to do, or mad supervisors twisting our melons, the hours were longer and there was less time off. We were open seven days a week, fourteen hours a day, three hundred and sixty-five days a year.

And little things irritated. Like going to the other side of town to get a fresh batch of jasmine flowers, or waiting for the last table of customers to leave before closing, or another trip to the iceman or off-licence, emptying the ashtrays, sweeping the floor, wiping the tables, locking up, opening up. And although independently these things didn't amount to much, collectively they began to drive me slightly nuts.

25.

At first our neighbour in the Scandinavian restaurant, the Norwegian Orangutan, ignored me completely. His presence in our lives was mostly irrelevant and peripheral, but one day, as he swept leaves outside his restaurant, he addressed me directly for the first time. When this happened I was sitting outside the bar sipping an ice-cold beer and perusing the latest edition of the Bangkok Post.

'Hey, you, how your bar doing?'

I have never appreciated being referred to as 'you', and because of his previous unfriendly and uncooperative attitude my instinct was to tell the mug to fuck off. Yet, after a moment's reflection, I decided life was too short.

'Very bad mate, if it carries on like this we'll be bankrupt before Christmas.'

Surprised by my honesty the orangutan nodded sympathetically and then went into great detail about the problems Westerners face when running a small business in Thailand: difficult authorities, corrupt police and unfriendly locals to name just a few. He didn't mention anything about the trouble with his ex-wife and losing his home, and, being a sensitive soul I was considerate enough not to bring the subject up.

The downside to my social attitude was that from that point onwards the Norwegian spoke to me nearly every day. And boy could he moan. He moaned about everything in Sang Som. He moaned about Thai people, the Thai royal family, the government, his customers, the weather, the restaurant business and the tourist trade. In fact he moaned about everything and anything, all the time, but his biggest gripes were reserved exclusively for the women of Sang Som, and Thai women in general.

According to him they were the most manipulative and scheming women on the planet. If I were a clever fellow, he told me, I'd go home and marry a nice English girl. Yet he hadn't gone home and married a nice Norwegian girl, and was conducting a tawdry affair with one of his employees.

I was hanging out some washing on the rooftop of the bar when I caught him in the act. On pegging out my clothes some very particular noises could be heard from inside the Norwegian's little shed. Then, a few minutes later, one of the cleaners appeared from within. When she saw me I smiled and gave her a knowing wink and she scuttled away, embarrassed.

Also, for a cleaner she was very well dressed, a fact that hadn't gone unnoticed by the observant eye of Mindi. On seeing the cleaner stroll past the bar in a pair of new shoes, she shook her head.

'She more clean restaurant old Norway man, look her shoe, cost month salary an she three pair!'

Then there were the hookers. One day, as I was riding around town getting provisions for the bar, I passed my neighbour riding on the other side of the road. Perched on the back of his moped, long black hair flying in the wind, was a heavily made up Thai girl. She was wearing a pair of distinctive white thigh length leather boots.

I gave them a friendly wave and the girl waved back like she was still touting for business. As for Monkey boy he completely blanked me, looking straight ahead with a determined face. I didn't think anything of it until the next morning when the cleaner arrived to commence her shift. I was plotted up in my usual position, beer and Bangkok Post in hand.

Within seconds shouting and angry words erupted inside the Scandinavian restaurant. Then an object sailed through the air and landed a few feet in front of me with a resounding thud. It was a white thigh length leather boot. The boot was followed by the appearance of a girl, hopping on one leg, the same girl I'd seen riding on the back of the old man's moped.

There was a lot more shouting after that until the cleaner marched out with her nose in the air and disappeared up the street. Much later the old man surfaced and began sweeping the front of his restaurant in melancholy fashion. Feeling mischievous I asked if everything was all right.

The old man stopped sweeping. His face was drawn and haggard.

'Look here English, take my advice, get out of this town and get out of Thailand before it's too late, don't end up like me.'

Don't end up like him? I began to worry. I definitely didn't want to end up like him, but I wasn't ready to leave Sang Som or Thailand. I looked at the Norwegian man and his grim face, and realised I'd never seen him smile, not even once.

'Hey, d'ya ever think about going back to Norway?

The old man stopped sweeping and shot me a broken-hearted look, 'Everyday boy, everyday.'

26.

The days went by and by. Boring days, monotonous days, days that seemed like they might never end. After a few weeks, due to a lack of customers in the daytime, we were forced to let Pree go and put Nut and Pooh on part time hours.

None of them minded. Pree found work elsewhere and the other two landed day jobs. And yet Christmas was just around the corner. And as everyone involved in Sang Som's tourist industry kept telling us, things would pick up just before Christmas, the commencement of high season. From then until April business would boom.

The imminent advent of high season gave us hope, and Mindi took to saying the same sentence at least once a day. During extended lulls she would stand in the doorway of the bar, gaze out on the empty street, and announce wistfully. 'Yah, next month high season, make lot money, for sure we do.'

But until then we were barely surviving, just getting by, even though we had implemented a series of cost cutting measures.

After a particularly bad night, where we had taken just a few hundred Baht, Mindi picked up an imported bottle of Cointreau and looked at it in a forlorn manner.

'What?' I asked.

'Bottle empty, replace mus, ba expensive.'

'How much?'

'Nine hun-led baht.'

'How much we got?'

'Six hun-led.'

The profit to be earned from cocktails was huge, but we were being forced to spend the profits from the bar without replenishing our stocks, a short-term solution that could only lead to one thing.

'We'll just have to sell other cocktails until we can afford to replace the bottle,' I said.

Mindi tapped a finger against the empty bottle.

'No, replace now, ba no real one, fake one buy.'

'What d'ya mean, buy fake one?'

'Come, we drink shop, an me show.'

At the shop, Mindi explained that for every bottle of imported liquor or spirit there was a fake substitute manufactured in Thailand. The bottles were slightly different, but more importantly the contents cost less than half the price of the genuine article.

'Do they taste the same?' I said.

'Yah.'

We purchased a bottle of fake Cointreau for five hundred Baht, a massive saving, and when I opened the bottle and took a swig I couldn't tell the difference.

'Tastes identical.'

Mindi carefully poured the fake Cointreau into the old bottle, the real one, 'Yah, do every bottle same same,'

And we did. As every bottle of imported liquor and spirit was used up we replaced it with a moody one. None of our customers ever complained. The only spirit we couldn't replace was tequila because for some reason there was no fake tequila, an oversight by the producers of counterfeit goods.

27.

Despite all of our dodgy cost-saving measures we still struggled to make ends meet. Then, one morning as I debated whether to have my first beer of the day, Mindi returned from a shopping trip highly excited.

'Jo-Jo, Jo-Jo, good business come soon, good for bar an something me forget.'

I decided not to have a beer. It was a big decision.

'Why's that?'

'Why, vegetarian festival, tha why!'

I didn't see how a vegetarian festival was going to improve the fortunes of our bar. The veggie community just didn't have a reputation for producing hard drinkers, not unless you figured in carrot juice and smoothies.

'How's that gonna help?'

'Vegetarian famous festival world round, tourist many come Sang Som.'

'A vegetarian festival? But vegetarians don't drink; they're a bunch of health freaks.'

'Eeh, baa, ting tong! Everyone drink many drink, Thai people an farang, same every year.'

After that declaration Mindi gave me the low down. According to her the festival occurred every year on the first day of the ninth Chinese lunar month and lasted for a duration of nine days. The origins of the festival were shrouded in mystery, but a commonly held belief was that it was brought to Thailand around two hundred years before by a group of wandering Chinese minstrels. Mindi became reverential, even somewhat pious as she relayed the story to me.

'An minstrels fell ill malaria on Phuket islan, an for cure wen on strict veg diet nine days an nine nights, praying tha nine emperor gods ensure healthy mine an bo-dee.'

'Did the cure work?'

'Yah, minstrel cure an live happy after. Now Thai people hold festival ev-ree year to honour nine emperor gods.'

'Sounds groovy.'

'Yah, during tha time, people mus keep body clean, wear white, yah an must be-have, no meat, no sex, no al-co-hol.'

'No alcohol, I thought you said everyone drinks?'

'No jelly brain, only festival people do, all rest people big par-tee.'

'You had me going there for a minute.'

Mindi continued. 'An light lantern an go many temple, an stick knife an spear in body, ba no hurt.'

'How can they not get hurt if they stick a spear into themselves?'

'I no sure, thing do hurt. Last year my friend put spear in mouth. So I ask, I say do hurt, an say no, ba next day he hos-pital.'

But whatever the vagaries of the festival's roots and rituals the tourist numbers in Sang Som doubled and the whole town adopted a party atmosphere. Unfortunately, despite a hundred per-cent increase in tourism, business in the bar remained slack. After the second day of the festival, as we watched another lantern-led procession pass gaily by, we came to the sad conclusion that the event wasn't going to provide us with any extra custom.

We watched glumly as the worshippers let off round after round of firecrackers.

'I no under-stan,' cried Mindi above the din, 'many people, ba none our bar.'

'No, none our bar,' repeated Nut and Pooh like a couple of pretty parrots.

'That's coz these travellers are not here to drink, they're here to eat vegetables. Whoever thought a vegetarian festival would im-prove custom needs their head examined,' I grumbled, somewhat unfairly, fishing for an argument just to pass the time, and yet no response was forthcoming. The girls were all smiling manically. I turned around, clocked what had caused the strange behaviour, and went into automatic customer mode.

Due to my dodgy visa situation I'd been instructed by Mindi to behave exactly like a customer whenever the authorities showed their face. And there, standing little more than three feet away, were two uniformed police officers. Although a partner in the bar, I possessed only a thirty-day transit visa, and if caught working on this visa I was going to be in trouble, big trouble, and an enforced stay in the Monkey House or Bangkok Hilton was not on my 'Things to do while in Thailand' list.

While Nut and Pree attended to the needs of the officers, a disorientated lone traveller stumbled into the bar. To make my customer pose appear more realistic, I grabbed the traveller's arm.

'Take a seat mate,' I urged, in a friendly voice.

'Cheers,' said the traveller.

'D'ya wanna a beer?' I said loudly, mostly for the benefit of the policemen, who were now seated at a table directly behind me.

The traveller nodded and I ordered another beer from Pooh. One of the officers, who looked like an Asian version of a young Elvis, pulled out a handgun. This freaked me, but I played it cool, took a nonchalant swig of beer, and introduced myself to the drunken traveller.

'What's your name amigo?'

'Marvin,' slurred the traveller.

'And where ya from?'

Marvin took a slurp from his beer.

'Isle of Man.'

I'd never met anyone from the Isle of Man before, but as Marvin drunkenly explained what he was doing in Sang Som, I contemplated my visa situation. On entering Thailand my battered passport had been stamped with an automatic transit visa valid for thirty-days. If I wished to stay on longer in the country said transit visa had to be renewed each month, and anyone wishing to do so without leaving the country was forced to embark on a bureaucratic process that was both comical and absurd.

My situation entailed travel to the nearest Thai/Malaysian border at a place called Pedang Besar. Once there I had to cross over the border into No Man's Land, receive an exit stamp, then walk a few feet and re-cross the same border whereupon I received another automatic thirty-day transit visa.

The whole trip was a gruelling fifteen-hour bus ride and a common scam utilised by travellers looking to extend their stay in Thailand without going to an embassy or leaving the country entirely. The visa situation was another reason why I considered my stay in Thailand to be a temporary one. There had to be a limit to how many times I could do the border run before one of the guards recognised my spaced out face. If that happened I would be open to all sorts of bribes, petty corruption, and tricky situations. At best the border run was a time-consuming and expensive mission and at worse, well I didn't care to think about that.

Marvin was still talking.

'She's on my bike.'

'She's what?'

Marvin pointed to Mindi's moped.

'That Thai girl, she's taken my wheels, you know one of those.'

'Oh, you mean a moped?'

Marvin took a long, slow swig of beer.

'Yeah, she borrowed it and disappeared.'

'Who's she?'

'The Thai girl.'

'Which Thai girl?'

'The one with long black hair.'

I looked from side to side and pointed to Nut, Pooh and Mindi. They all had long glossy black hair.

'You mean like them?'

Marvin screwed up his eyes and craned his neck forward like an old chicken.

'Yeah just like them.'

'Well, that narrows it down.'

Marvin hiccupped and looked at me like an insane person might. Then, still grinning manically, he attempted a swig from his bottle, but only succeeded in pouring beer all down his front. His next move was to wipe his wet tee shirt with one hand and attempt to place his bottle on the table in front of him, but he missed the table, not by much, a matter of millimetres, but enough for the bottle to smash onto the ground.

Marvin apologised, but the sound of breaking glass caught the attention of the two policemen. The Elvis officer said something to Mindi and pointed to our table. I tried to act normal, but whenever you try to act normal you always end up acting like some subnormal freak. After a brief dialogue with Elvis, Mindi disappeared inside the bar. She returned moments later holding a plastic mug. She placed the mug in front of Marvin.

'Here kind sir, need, yah?'

Marvin looked into the mug, saw it was full of beer, and took a swig.

Mindi leant up close and whispered in my ear.

'It okay, police friend, just free drink them.'

'What?'

'All bars police free drink them, this normal, this Thai style.'

A tense hour and several drinks later, the policemen finally left. Not long after a new Thai girl appeared on the scene. She was riding a moped. I'd never seen her before. Marvin pointed in the girl's direction.

'That's her.'

The girl jumped off the moped and took off her crash helmet. She placed the yellow helmet on our table, unclipped her hair, and shook it free until some of it went in my eyes. The girl gave my arm a gentle squeeze.

'Solly,' she whispered, huskily.

'No worries,' said I.

As soon as the girl saw Mindi she let out an exaggerated scream and they fell into each other's arms. After they had settled down Mindi introduced us.

'This my friend Nicole, live Phuket, me know long, long time.'

'Hi Nicole,' I replied languidly.

Nicole flashed me a glamorous smile. 'Hi.' Then she looked at the state of Marvin and the plastic mug, 'Marvin why still drink? Drink lot already.'

Marvin looked up, hiccupped again, and commenced to sleep where he sat.

Nicole frowned.

'I thing Marvin alco-holic.'

'Yah all British tourist drink lot,' said Mindi.

'An British women,' replied Nicole, looking superior.

'Yah, British man an woman, drink how you say, like fish.'

I didn't bother defending my fellow countrymen from the lush accusations. They couldn't be disputed. Brits comfortably out drank all other nations bar none. It was something I felt vaguely proud about.

While Marvin slept, the conversation turned to the fortunes of the business. Mindi was worried.

'It bad Nicole, no good business an tough time.'

'Need entertainment, something make bar excite. What bout karaoke?' suggested Nicole.

'Many karaoke already, too rival much.'

Nicole leaned in close to Mindi and spoke exclusively in Thai. The girls burst out laughing.

'No we no do, we no do, Nicole you bad girl, bad, bad girl.'

I felt excluded. 'What did she say?'

'She say, why we no girls from Phuket, working girl, can use room upstairs.'

Now it was my turn to smile. 'Sounds like a groovy idea.'

'You shut up, that dir-tee.'

'Why, it could work, what's the problem?'

Nicole came and put an arm around me. 'Listen Jo-Jo Mindi, he know good idea when hear one.'

Mindi was disgusted. 'Over my body dead, no we must thing something better.'

Just then a crowd of tourists gathered to watch another festival procession. None of them came into the bar, a depressing spectacle. Yet, as I observed how the tourists delighted in the cultural attraction an idea came to me.

'That's how we'll get some punters in our bar,' I announced excitedly.

'How we do?' said Mindi.

'Don't you see?' I said, 'we need to make the bar a cultural attraction.'

'How we do?'

'We start by serving vegetarian food as part of the festival?'

'No, need license, an no time get one,' said Mindi sadly.

'Yah I know, I know wha do, do traditional Thai dancing, all tourist like.' said Nicole.

Instantly I knew it was a good idea and so did Mindi. Thai Dancing. It was obvious. All we had to do was get hold of some traditional Thai folk music, obtain traditional outfits, advertise the show on flyers, and employ some dancers.

'But who can do the dance?' I said.

Nicole threw back her head and fluttered her eyelashes.

'Me!'

'Do you know how to perform traditional dancing?'

'All Thai people know, we learn in the time of childhood.'

Mindi was totally energised and immediately back to her old self, the old self that had so attracted me in the beginning.

'Come Nicole, we music an dress.'

An hour later the girls returned to the Buddha Bar laden with shopping bags.

'Now me show you traditional Thai dancing,' announced Nicole confidently.

Mindi handed me a CD.

'Put on music, Nicole dance.'

Whilst Nicole got ready, I went inside the bar and put the music on. The traditional music sounded like a cat singing under-water, yet it was authentic enough. After some time Nicole appeared dressed in a traditional sari. The dress had an oriental elegance to it, hugging Nicole's voluptuous figure, and accentuating her many curves. She proudly displayed herself and we clapped and cheered.

As the music played Nicole struck a traditional pose, but then something strange happened. The music was slow paced and seemed to demand an elegant artistic dance, but instead Nicole erupted into a frenzied series of sexual gyrations. Traditional Thai dancing, it was more akin to the Lambada!

I stopped the music.

'What the fuck was that?' I said.

'Yeah, wha that? Look like pat pong bar girl,' said Mindi.

'Wha? You wan tourist, an every tourist like sex, so dance sexy.'

'But we're trying to get the culture vultures, not those wanting to go to a lap-dancing club,' I said and gave Nicole a wink, 'but I have to admit that was a very sexy dance.'

Nicole smiled glamorously.

'I know, all men love me dance, I copy film Dirty Dancing.'

'Yes all men love, an you many men,' said Mindi, at which both girls commenced a very vocal argument.

While this was all going on, Pooh began showing Nut her own take on traditional Thai dancing. I watched carefully. It was exactly the sort of dancing we'd been talking about and how I'd envisaged it might look. I told Mindi and Nicole to shut up and gestured to Pooh.

'I think Pooh knows how to do it, look.'

Mindi and Nicole stopped shouting and looked to Pooh who immediately became self-conscious. Nut gave her a nudge.

'Pooh show us your dance,' I said.

Reluctantly, after much persuasion, Pooh stood up. I turned the drowning cat music back on and something beautiful happened. The pretty young girl performed a very elegant and attractive demonstration of traditional dancing right before our amazed eyes. Even Nicole grudgingly admitted that Pooh could dance.

'Yah she dance good, but no Thai dance, tha dance from Laos,' she moaned.

I didn't care if the dance came from Timbuktu because we had found our dancer. Without further ado I asked Pooh if she would dance, but she just shook her pretty head and laughed. Then Mindi mentioned payment and her whole demeanour underwent a transformation. Within seconds she agreed to be our traditional dancer. With no time to lose Pooh's debut performance was scheduled for the following evening.

28.

I woke early the next morning, just before noon, and after showering climbed onto the rooftop to hang some washing out to dry. When that was done I sat on the parapet of the rooftop, smoked a cigarette, and surveyed the scene. Normally I don't like to smoke in the morning, but this morning felt different, like a special day, a day full of promise, eastern promise. So I smoked a cigarette and gazed at the view.

The landmark peaks of Khao Khnap Nam rose upwards like two green fangs, while the lazy Sang Som River slid effortlessly between them and out into the lazy Andaman Sea. In the distance fishing boats bobbed here and there. I thought about the fishermen on those little boats. On a day like today it seemed an ideal job, just cast out the net, sit back, relax, and wait for the catch.

It was another hot one and the sun shone down with extra special tropical ferocity. There were blue skies all around and the jungle clad mountains surrounding Sang Som stood out, defined against the blue like a herd of green elephants.

Above the mountains cumulus clouds tumbled across the sky creating a series of mad shapes and figures. I gazed wistfully at the mountains, and the sky, and the river, and the sea, but neglected to gaze at the sun because it was too bright, but I felt its warmth and power and its innate goodness.

The streets below bustled with human activity, another busy day for industrious people, and for idlers like myself a day to spend on the riverbank, daydreaming of a lost love or an old friend lost along the way. But today there was no time for idleness because there was work to be done, like advertising the bar's new attraction, Traditional Thai Dancing.

We spent the afternoon handing out flyers to as many tourists as possible. When that was done we completed all our usual tasks. We went to the market for fresh fruit and jasmine flowers. We paid the iceman and beer man. We visited the supermarket and the bottle shop and made sure the bar was looking spick and span. Then we waited.

The first dance was scheduled for eight o'clock and, miraculously, at five to eight the bar was full and each customer had been served a drink. I gave Pooh the signal and slipped the traditional folk music on.

The submerged cat began wailing and Pooh emerged nervously from the kitchen. She took one look at all the faces packed into the tiny bar, spun around, and ran back from whence she had came. Stage fright. Mindi went after her, rapidly followed by myself.

In the kitchen Mindi remonstrated loudly with Pooh, who in turn looked petrified.

'What's the problem?' I asked.

'Scared all people, say no dance.'

Pooh was shaking. In that state it didn't seem possible that she would be able to perform. We had to think on our feet and come up with a solution. I grabbed a bottle of vodka along with a shot glass and handed them to Mindi.

'Give her two shots of that, maybe three, it will calm her nerves.'

Pooh backed away into a corner and clamped a hand across her mouth. Mindi stepped forward, grim determination on her visage. I caught Pooh's eye and gave her a friendly smile and the thumbs up, but she looked at me like I'd just sold her into slavery.

It appeared to be a stalemate an impasse until Mindi suddenly barked at Pooh in bullet Thai, the ferocity and speed of which caught Pooh unawares. Next she grabbed Pooh by the hair, tipped her head back, pinched her nose betwixt finger and thumb, and poured a shot of vodka down her throat. Then she clamped a hand across her mouth. Pooh scrunched up her eyes, gagged, and made a strange gurgling noise not dissimilar to a death rattle.

When she was sure the operation was a success Mindi took her hand away. Pooh wobbled on her feet and coughed weakly.

'Is she all right?' I asked, taken aback by Mindi's roughhouse tactics.

Mindi nodded and poured another shot of vodka. Resigned to her fate and warmed by the alcohol Pooh became stoical. She nonchalantly held back her head and thrust a shaky arm out.

After the third shot it was a breeze. With confidence levels boosted sky high by the alcohol, Pooh walked into the bar like a prima ballerina and knocked the audience out with a dance to warm the cockles of any travel-hardened heart. She floated from table to table like a lover in a dream, her eyes sparkled under the spotlight, her glossy onyx hair swished and swayed, and her elegant sarong glittered like the dress of a debutante.

She finished her dance with a graceful curtsey, her hands spiralling to the heavens like strange exotic butterflies, while the bar erupted into a loud and lengthy applause. For a few magical moments all the men were in love and all the women wanted to be Pooh or take up Thai dancing as a hobby, and as she returned for a third encore the Buddha Bar was back in business.

29.

Later on, as I stuffed an excellent night's takings into the statue of Buddha, I felt very good. Mindi was visibly happy, back to her old self, talking animatedly, laughing and smiling. And I reckoned all a person needs to carry on is a little bit of money, good health, and a fistful of hope.

For the rest of the Chinese vegetarian festival we were busy every night, and by the end we had taken more money in one week than in the whole of the previous month. These were heady days for the bar, the salad days, no more waiting anxiously for customers to turn up; no more worrying about how the rent would be paid, the staff, the beer man, the iceman, and whether the fateful day might arrive when we couldn't afford to eat.

During this prosperous period my relationship with Mindi blossomed and my relationship with my immediate environment improved. I was more friendly and good-natured with my fellow man and beast alike. I became tolerant of the customers and their annoying ways, even laughing at some of their wearying traveller tales, the same ones I'd heard a thousand times before.

The cash injection had a liberating effect. For the first time in months we were able to head to the nearest department store and splash out on some new clothes. I bought a tee shirt and a pair of shorts and Mindi bought a pair of shoes and an embroidered denim skirt. We could even afford a few luxuries and I persuaded Mindi to buy a crate of white wine, imported from France.

I pictured myself sitting outside the bar, supping chilled wine in the purple evening, nodding to customers as they entered the bar, and then signalling to one of the waitresses to tend to their needs. I wouldn't get up myself because I would be too busy thinking of ways to invest all the profits from the bar, a plasma TV perhaps, or a pool table.

So for a while everything was hunky dory and we even bagged our first regulars, Nicole and Marvin. They visited each evening. Nicole was an all round good time girl, one of a breed of Thai women that prey on older Western men looking for love, companionship, and maybe even a wife. Although no beauty and a divorced single mother, Nicole possessed what can only be defined as sex appeal, and those lonely, sex starved, loveless men that flocked to Thailand in their thousands were legitimate and easy targets.

During this time she had four Western men on the go, all of whom were convinced that she was in love with them. After having promised to marry each one and live with them in their country of birth, the mugs sent money to her each week or month. In this way she led a very comfortable lifestyle and was able to afford private education for her child, and send money to her extended family, including ex-husband and boyfriends.

After Mindi gave me the low down I asked how she was going to swing it.

'So Nicole, what ya gonna do if all your boyfriends manage to sort out your visa at exactly the same time as each other?'

Nicole shot me a dismissive look and gave her elaborately painted finger nails a close inspection.

'Wha you mean?'

Marvin looked up from his plastic mug.

'He means, Nicole, that four men is like four cocks, and that's a lot of cock for such a small woman.'

Nicole narrowed her eyes.

'Shut up Marvin, you jus dwink, I talking Jo-Jo.'

'What I mean Nicole is which one will you go with when they ask you to live with them in Europe?'

Nicole fluttered her eyelashes.

'Tha easy, tha man love me most.'

At this Marvin choked on his beer.

'So really the one with the most money wins the contest,' I said.

Nicole laughed and kicked me under the table.

'Eeh, bah ting tong!'

Marvin on the other hand was an enigma. From conversation it was obvious he had been travelling alone for years without any visible means of support, and without any recognisable itinerary. A creature of habit, he slept most of the day, before appearing at the bar each evening whereupon he would get slowly sloshed.

For the first few hours he stuck to bottled beer and after about ten of those switched to gin and tonics. After four or five of those he would start popping tranquillisers. I got to know when he was lashed because he would offer me a tranquilliser from a stash he kept in a plastic bag. If in the mood I would pop one or two, or save them for the next morning, as I'd discovered they were an excellent hangover cure. They took the edge off.

Marvin bought his pills from a chemist in town and by my reckoning was popping around ten to fifteen a day. Despite the amount of alcohol he imbibed each night, and the massive pill intake, he was well behaved at all times. He was never rowdy or argumentative, even when so incapacitated he became incoherent. After a week I decided he'd either won the lottery, was the recipient of a trust fund, or had robbed a bank.

30.

On the last day of the festival it began to rain. It seemed like a bad omen. When I say it began to rain, what I mean is that the heavens opened, and when I say the heavens opened, what I really mean is that they opened and stayed open 24/7.

A few days later Marvin and I were seated outside the bar watching the rain when a large procession from the vegetarian festival appeared on the horizon. Usually the processions passed by without turning down our little road, but on this occasion the procession headed straight towards the bar.

'Look, the procession's heading straight for us,' I said.

'Yep.' said Marvin.

An open truck swamped in yellow banners, the primary colour of the festival, was followed by about thirty or more veggie freaks. Most of the participants had gone into a trance-like state, heads rocking rapidly from side to side, eyes rolling into their heads. As they marched along they chanted and mutilated themselves. One extremist had slashed his chest with a huge machete and his body glistened in the rain, sweat and blood shimmering on an athletic bronzed torso. Another had pierced a spear through both cheeks. The scene was both stunning and disturbing.

On top of the truck, stood a man dressed all in white. This goon chanted into a megaphone and waved his arms around a good deal. Staff watching from next door's disco began screaming. They fell to their knees and covered their heads with their hands. Just as I was wondering why they had reacted in such a manner a battery of ear-splitting firecrackers was let off, endless machine-gun-like rounds popping here there and everywhere.

After initially jumping out of my skin, I composed myself and took a slow swig of beer. Marvin hiccupped and offered me his bag of pills. I took two, a yellow and a pink, just as a firecracker zipped past my eyebrow.

'Easy,' I said.

Marvin hiccupped again and his eyes widened.

'Look at that one!'

I zoned in and was presented with an unbelievable sight, a veggie with a bicycle framed pierced through both cheeks.

'Mother,' I said, as a firecracker hit me on the shoulder and ricocheted into Marvin's beer.

31.

Ten days later it was still raining and a basket of washing I'd originally hung out to dry ten days previously was wetter than when I first put it on the line. Monsoon conditions. I took to walking around and quoting the bard.

'The rain it raineth every day,' I said to anyone who cared to listen, but no one did, they just looked at me strangely. Anyway, despite Shakespeare, the atrocious weather contributed to a drastic decline in tourist numbers. Once more we were reduced to the miserable condition of sitting outside the bar, waiting anxiously for customers to arrive. Yet, time and time again, they never showed. The bar remained empty, drinks were never drunk, music echoed sadly off the walls, and even the Buddha mural appeared more sympathetic looking than usual. It was demoralising.

Luckily Marvin was still gracing us with his presence. His individual drinks consumption and subsequent cash expenditure was equivalent to five paying customers, but as the bad weather continued he spoke of moving on. It had us worried. Without his custom we would be back to pre-festival takings, and the prospects of the bar became as gloomy as the terrible weather.

On the third day of downpours Mindi had a brainwave. The great idea was to take a trip to the Chao Fa pier and ask a local fisherman when the rain would end. If anyone knew when a break in the awful weather would occur it would be someone whose livelihood depended on it she told us confidently. I agreed and we set off immediately.

At Chao Fa pier we found an especially weather-beaten looking individual, holed up inside the cabin of a long tail boat. Mindi approached and posed the question. Seemingly glad to be asked, the old sea dog jumped out of his ancient vessel and scanned the horizon.

After a few minutes of this he grabbed a stick and drew a circle in the muddy shore three times before throwing the stick into the river. After gazing at the stick until it was out of sight he turned around. Then he said something in Thai, smiled, and returned to the shelter of his boat.

'What'd he say?' I asked Mindi.

'He say fon tok end before new sun.'

'You mean tomorrow?'

'Yah.'

'D'ya think he knows what he's talking about?'

'Yah, yah. He ole time fisherman, he wise same Lord Buddha.'

Armed with that indisputable information we walked away feeling glad in our hearts, but funnily enough three days later it was still raining.

The following evening I was sitting outside the bar with Marvin. He was the only customer and the rain was so heavy it danced off the roads and pavements. The girls were elsewhere. Surrounding our table were four mosquito coils. I felt a leg tingle and shot my arm out in bullet fashion. Afterwards I inspected my hand. A dead mosquito lay squished inside. I inspected the afflicted leg, a red welt already appearing, just below the knee.

'Fuck it, gonna have to get some more coils,' I said, as I grabbed a small tin of tiger balm from a selection on the table and rubbed some of the pungent jelly into the fresh insect bite.

Marvin glanced at the coils and slapped a hand down hard on his neck.

'You'd think four would be enough,' he said.

I eyeballed the thunderous sheet of rain. 'It's this damned fon tok, the mosquito population has exploded.'

Marvin pulled out a small can of insect repellent and handed it to me. 'Here try this, it's jungle-proof.'

I took the can and sprayed myself all over. The fumes entered my mouth and took my breath away. 'Cheers,' I croaked.

Five minutes later I felt another tingle and the ominous buzzing of the irrepressible critters. I jumped up and shook myself down. 'Jesus Christ, I don't think I can stand it anymore!'

Marvin raised his bottle of Chang beer and took two or three long pulls. 'Go easy, keep drinking, the poisonous qualities of alcohol will eventually protect you.'

I grabbed my latest beer bottle and downed the contents in one swig.

'I think you could be right. I read somewhere that excessive alcohol intake combats any form of infectious disease.'

'Yeah, sure does, way more effective than malaria pills.'

'Possibly not so great for the liver, though.'

Marvin smiled. 'A minor drawback. Can I have another Chang please?'

As I fetched the beers I decided something would have to be done about the mossies. It wouldn't be easy. The mosquito of the tropics is a particularly ferocious and superior type of mosquito. They proved the old adage, that they only bite from dusk until dawn, to be utterly false. These super mossies attacked 24/7. They were relentless.

Although a Buddhist philosophy of mine was to treat all living creatures as sacred, mosquitoes were a notable exception. As far as I was concerned the fuckers were evil. I grabbed the beers and returned to my spot opposite Marvin and handed him a bottle.

'You know, what gets me is their ability to survive whatever I throw at them. Each evening I light plenty of mosquito coils and place them strategically around the bar, but it fails to stop the guer-rillas.'

'The guerrillas?'

'Yeah, the clever fuckers. If they don't bite you in the bar, they wait in the bedrooms and ambush you in the dead of night.'

'Have you tried a mosquito net?'

'Don't like em, make me claustrophobic. Instead, I do a mossie check just before hitting my pit. I take no mercy, but a few always evade my nightly massacre.'

'Maybe you need to be more Zen about the matter.'

'More Zen?'

'Yeah, chill out, let the fuckers do their worst.'

'Do their worst? Just this morning I counted seventeen fresh bites!'

Marvin winced, 'sounds horrific.'

'It is, but you know what?'

'What?'

'The other night, after an especially murderous blitz, I col-lapsed onto my bed exhausted from all the killing.'

'So what?'

'Get this. The next day I awoke with my right fist tightly shut.'

'And?'

'And when I opened it, lying there in the palm of my hand was the enemy, a mosquito, dead as a doornail.'

'Shit.'

'And as I stared at the tiny insect, lying there in the palm of my hand, I felt an overwhelming empathy towards my old foe.'

'You did?'

'I did. It had only been trying its best to survive in this cruel world, only living according to its evolutionary survival plan.'

'So what did you do?'

I stood up and walked over to where a large plant pot was situated at the entrance to the bar. 'I decided it was only right and proper the mosquito received its last rites. I buried it in this plant pot here, even marking its grave with a small cross.'

Marvin joined me at the plant pot. The cross was there, stuck in the dirt. Some writing had been carved into the cross by me, a sort of dedication.

'What does it say?' said Marvin.

'Sacred to the memory of Bert who died.'

'Bert?'

'He kinda looked like a Bert.'

32.

Along with the increased mosquito population the rain forced another unwelcome guest to seek new, higher, drier, living arrangements. The first I became aware of the enforced migration was on being awakened one morning by a loud, ear-piercing scream.

Fearing that Mindi's husband had returned to complete some unfinished business, I grabbed Karl's Special Forces knife from under the pillow, and headed downstairs. Just before I got to the kitchen Mindi appeared, waving her hands above her head and stomping her feet.

I grabbed her by the waist, and held the knife out in front, ready to defend both of us.

'Is it your husband?'

'Wha?'

I backed us away from the kitchen like we were in a three-legged race.

'Is it your husband, in the kitchen?'

Mindi started laughing.

'My hus-ban, no, no my hus-ban,'

I relaxed my grip. Then Mindi changed her mind.

'Yah, my hus-ban, an all fam-ily.'

'What?'

'Come see.'

Mindi's light-hearted manner meant it was impossible for her husband to be hiding in the kitchen. Once inside everything was revealed. Mindi repeated a Thai word over and over.

'See, how say English, I thing rat.'

I eyeballed the bottom of the fridge. A large pink tail was sticking out, a tail that could only belong to one animal.

'That's a rat, a fucking big one as well.'

'Yah rat, juss like my hus-ban.'

'Is it dead?'

'No, alive, many more, rest drain down.'

I kicked the side of the fridge. The tail didn't budge. If it wasn't a dead rat, it was a defiant one. Mindi indicated something more constructive should be done by glaring at me. I got down on all fours to get a closer look, but as I did a furry ball of fur shot out over my head and run straight down my back. I screamed in fright and jumped to my feet. Mindi was in hysterics.

'It's not funny,' I bawled.

'Yah, funny, never fast you move.'

After this episode it continued to rain and the rats didn't go away like we hoped, and if anything their numbers increased. Mindi was unconcerned.

'When fon-tok stop, rat back drain down.'

Somehow I didn't think so. There was a plentiful supply of food and drink in the bar. And if, like me, those rats liked a drink they would be mad to leave. The only answer was poison and I set out to obtain some at once.

On the way I did some research in a nearby internet café. A list of facts presented themselves before my freaked optics. There are five rats for every human being on earth. I scratched my chin, assumed the pose of an underdog, and compared the pictures on the website to the mental image of the rats from the bar. It became obvious we were dealing with the brown rat, otherwise known as the common rat, or rattus vulgaris.

I reeled off some impressive stats. The average brown rat can grow to a size of 20 inches from nose to tail, possesses iron-like teeth comparable to steel, and is capable of exerting pressures of up to 7,000 pounds per square inch.

Now things really got worrying. Male and female rats could fuck up to 20 times per day. Compared with my best ever performance of ten it was impressive. It was also possible for a dominant male rat to mate with up to twenty female rats in just six hours. The gestation period for a pregnant female was 21 days, the average litter between eight to ten pups.

I signalled to a girl working in the shop to hand me a calculator and made some calculations. By my estimation a single female rat was capable of producing 12 litters a year, with each litter containing up to twenty baby rats. With shaking hands I made further calculations. One pair of rats had the potential to produce 15,000 descendants in a single year!

Then I read the killer stat, the stat to make you have sleepless nights. Rats carry disease, even more diseases than the dreaded mosquito! Just looking at the list made feel ill; Weil's disease, Salmonella, Tuberculosis, Cryptosporidiosis, E.Coli, Foot and Mouth, Black Death. I read the symptoms of each disease and then wished I hadn't because it appeared I was suffering from each and every one.

I broke out into a cold sweat and ran out of the shop to buy some industrial strength rat poison. Before long I was armed with enough poison to kill a small country's worth of vermin. I returned to the bar, laid the poison down according to the strict instructions, and waited.

33.

Still it rained. The word for rain in Thai is fon tok and this period of relentless downpours became known in Sam Song as the Great Fon Tok. The townsfolk began to forget what the sun looked like, and for a few, especially the very young, earth's nearest star became a distant memory, something not to be believed in like a fairy tale or myth.

Meanwhile, laying down industrial strength rat poison didn't eradicate our little problem. Once digested the poison worked as a powerful anticoagulant and the afflicted rodents became groggier and groggier before slowly bleeding to death.

It was a particularly gruesome way to die and often a condemned rodent would wobble across the floor of the bar, blinking its eyes in a ponderous fashion, looking for somewhere to curl up and die. I became wracked with guilt. I was a murderer, a tyrant, an evil oppressor. Yet, the deed had been done and the rats had to die.

Keeping the doomed rodents out of view of the paying customers became a full-time occupation. Often a rat would appear out of nowhere and at the most inopportune times. Like when the bar was packed out with customers or during a performance of traditional Thai dancing, ponderous beady eyes searching in vain for some kind of ratty salvation. When this happened I would order one of the girls to create a diversion, while I disposed of the evidence.

But like the old saying goes, every cloud has a silver lining, and despite all the negatives the never ending downpours provided us with some custom we wouldn't have normally enjoyed. For as well as driving the rat population onto higher ground the weather also drove large numbers of rock climbing and scuba diving folk into town.

The nearby islands were deluged. Unable to pursue their favoured activities large groups arrived in Sang Som in search of alternative entertainment. Never one to miss an opportunity Mindi decided to hold an extreme sports party in the bar. The idea was simple. We re-worded the flyers, offered half-price cocktails to any scuba divers and rock climbers, and hoped some might show up.

A couple of days later a large group of travellers appeared on the horizon. They stopped a few feet from the bar, issued some disapproving looks, and talked amongst each other in conspirator tones. It was evident they were reluctant to come inside. Aside from the red neon Buddha sign the bar didn't have much going for it. It was tiny for one thing. The travellers remained in dither mode, they were young, athletic, and dressed exactly the same as each other.

Accompanying me outside the bar was Marvin.

'Scuba divers?' mumbled The Marv.

'And rock climbers,' I replied sleepily.

Although the bar was empty, and we were desperate for custom, I was in such an apathetic state of mind that the effort required to persuade any potential punters inside was beyond me. Instead I strolled lazily into the bar, informed Mindi there were some travellers outside, and played some dance music on the sound system.

In complete contrast to my apathy, Mindi immediately went to work in energetic fashion. Within five minutes, despite much shaking of heads and pointing in other directions, the group was inside our bar, ushered in by the irrepressible Mindi.

As Mindi strutted her stuff, it became obvious I was surplus to requirements. This feeling had been growing on me for a while. Instead of an asset to the bar I was a burden, drinking all the stocks, putting large dents in the meagre takings, and generally not helping out much. I wasn't sure how much I was drinking, but week-by-week my alcohol consumption had steadily increased.

Some idea of the scale of the problem hit home one night when four Dutch travellers made a request for Amstel beer. I remember Mindi running in excitedly and saying:

'Hey, four tourist, wan Am-stel!'

I was standing in the DJ area putting on a Northern Soul CD and supping from a bottle of Amstel. I remember looking at the bottle and wondering how many I'd drunk when Mindi cried out in dismay.

'Why, why no Am-stel.'

A few days before we had taken delivery of two crates of the stuff, so if none remained it meant I'd drunk forty-eight bottles in less than three days.

I hid the bottle I was supping from behind the counter and pretended to be engrossed in sorting what CD to play next. I remembered all this vividly because when Mindi discovered it was me who had drunk all the Amstel she shot me a look of contempt. And although she had been angry with me before, for a fleeting moment a primordial hatred appeared in those big brown eyes.

As thoughts of my own ineptitude flitted through my mind, I decided to turn over a new leaf and get energised. To kick off my helpfulness regime I played host with the most and interacted with our new customers with great enthusiasm. I went round each table asking them what music they would like to listen to, if they knew where the toilet was, etc. Then I sat down at a random table and introduced myself.

They were four rock climbers from California. After intros I feigned interest in the sport and listened to the conversation going down. It went something like this.

'Dude, that last route was a smooth send.'

'Shit, my arm's still pumped and I did an Elvis.'

'You gotta learn to stem more dude, I say it was a smooth send.'

'It was only a smooth send because we had the beta on it.'

'Dude, because of this damned fon tok I can't even remember that send it was so long ago, beta or no beta.'

'When this weather changes, we go on-sight!'

At this the rock climbers nodded their heads solemnly and repeated the word, on-sight, like a mantra.

I listened carefully, but understood nothing. They were speaking a foreign language.

'Are you people serious?' I asked.

The four rock climbers eyeballed me.

'I mean, what're ya talking about? I can't understand a word of it.'

The rock climbers exchanged knowing glances.

'You never climbed, buddy?'

121

'Na.'

'Maybe you need a translation?'

'Give it to me.'

At that the rock climbers translated the mysteries of rock-climbing jargon for my benefit. Although they were willing to share this esoteric knowledge, as soon as they did my life force began to slowly ebb away, and it wasn't long before I looked for an opportunity to escape. Luckily Pooh provided me with the perfect excuse when she dropped a glass. I stood up.

'Hey, hey, excuse me people, but I like that rock climbing argot especially Doing An Elvis. I'll remember that one and Chicken Head.'

As I edged away the rock climbers resumed another conspirator convo.

'What about Zane when he gripped on the banana ship?'

After that I passed a table of scuba divers from New Zealand and overheard scuba diving being described as a sport. It surprised me that anyone could describe scuba diving as a sport because I'd always considered the activity to be more of an aimless leisure pursuit, like jet-skiing or golf.

I introduced myself and listened in on the convo.

'Listen bro, our sport is safer than any other,' announced one, especially ardent character.

'Yeah bro, but how do you clarify the meaning of safe? I think if you check your dictionary you'll find the definition of safe is risk free,' replied his equally ardent mate.

'Don't give me that dictionary shit. Safe and risk free, they don't necessarily mean the same thing. Diving is safe, but it is not risk free. I mean like fuck, nothing is risk free. Getting out of bed is not risk free.'

'That's what I mean bro, diving is safe and no one should go around saying it isn't so.'

'How can you say it's safe when there are risks involved mate?'

'Shit, like you said there are risks involved in getting out of bed, walking, sleeping. Take driving for example, diving is much safer than driving.'

'Can you prove that?'

'Look at all the people killed on the roads each year.'

'True, but there are plenty more drivers than divers bro.'

As this serious, but banal, talk continued I yawned, felt a migraine coming on, and made my excuses. I wasn't missed.

Disillusioned by the disappointing start to my helpfulness regime I gave up, grabbed another beer from the fridge, a Heineken, and wandered out of the bar. Outside, Marvin had already reached the pill popping stage. He fumbled clumsily through his bag of tranquillisers.

'Wanna a pill,' he slurred.

I looked inside the bar, at all the scuba divers and rock-climbing freaks.

'Give me a red and a blue.'

Marvin handed me the pills.

'Anything interesting going on inside?'

I necked the pills.

'Nope.'

34.

The next morning I awoke to something remarkable. I rubbed my eyes and shook my head, but it didn't make any difference. Outside a brilliant blue sky and powerful white sunshine dominated the scene. Like a miracle the Great Fon Tok had finally abated, and with the break in the awful weather came the promise of prosperity and a brighter future.

The first thing that sprung to mind was the washing put out to dry on the rooftop many days ago. I dashed to the rooftop to inspect the long lost garments. There they were, my clothes, each item stiff as a board and brilliantly clean.

I cast an amazed eye over the town. In the devastating sunlight the buildings sparkled like polished gems. The entire town looked like it had been restored and far, far away, the sea glimmered. Fuck it, I decided to shut the bar and go to the beach. I hadn't been to the beach for ages and a sudden yearning for the smell of the ocean, cool water, and soft sea breezes gripped me.

The Rock Climbers and Scuba Divers had provided us with a bumper night and the long awaited high season was now just around the corner. If we could hold on until then the bar would make it, at least for another season, and everything would have been worthwhile. I took a deep breath of fresh sunlit air, picked up the plastic laundry basket, and rushed downstairs.

Inside the bedroom Mindi was asleep, but having kicked the sheet off, she lay naked with her legs spread open. I looked at her golden thighs and immediately got a hard on. I put the basket down in the corner of the room, undressed, and lay beside her sleeping form.

A mischievous and horny thought entered my head. I entertained the impish thought and then tried to stick my erect penis inside her. On the third prod Mindi awoke with a sleepy, yet startled yelp.

'Hey wha ya do?' she yawned.

'What?'

'You try put tha thing in me?'

'I did not.'

124

A sexy look came into Mindi's eyes and, without hesitating, she crawled over and placed my dick in her mouth.

'Or maybe I did,' I sighed and closed my eyes.

Afterwards, as we lay together in the afterglow, I told her my idea about closing the bar and going to the beach. Mindi licked her lips.

'Ba lose money when bar shut.'

I pointed to the basket of clean clothes. 'It's no longer raining.'

'Really, Great Fon-Tok end?'

'Yep, blue skies all over.'

'Okay we close bar an go lagoon beach.'

'Lagoon beach?'

Mindi kissed me.

'Beautiful baby'

We gave the girls a night off, packed our swimsuits, and jumped onto the moped. We rode for hours along small country roads, flanked either side by luxuriant green jungle and towering limestone cliffs. We stopped for a delicious yet simple meal at a small roadside restaurant. Hours passed. Eventually we came to a bumpy dirt track that wound its way through the jungle like a yellow snake.

We headed down the track until the lush green canopy gave way to blue skies and seagulls crying. And there it was, a shimmering emerald green lagoon, beyond which was a vast beach and swaying expanse of sea. The sands of the endless beach were dazzling white, the water slate grey and smooth as cut glass.

Apart from two fishermen, waist deep in water, the beach was deserted. I stripped down to my trunks and dived into the inviting water. The sea was so cool and calm that it felt like swimming in liquid silk and wonderfully refreshing after the long sweaty bike ride.

As I frolicked in the water the fishermen stopped fishing and returned to the beach. Mindi sat under the shade of a palm tree with her knees clasped against her bosom. I called out and did underwater handstands and she smiled and waved back. This is what it's all about, I told myself smugly. I floated on the water and

125

gazed at the sky and the clouds. I became lost in my own thoughts, until the sound of my name rudely awakened me from my cloud and sky reveries.

Mindi and the fishermen were standing together on the shoreline. They motioned for me to come out of the water. The wrinkled nut-brown men smoked hand rolled cigarettes and wore concerned expressions. I left the sea and walked over. One of the fishermen pointed at the sea and spoke to Mindi in the vernacular. They all laughed. Mindi slapped me gently on the shoulder.

'No swim, fish go, fish go.'

Only then did the penny drop. On that great deserted beach I had inconsiderately chosen to swim next to the only fisherman in sight, scaring away all the fish in the process.

The men wore straw hats to protect themselves from the sun and went barefoot. One of them gripped a white sack. I asked to look inside. Inside were three small fish. The way the fish lay there at the bottom of that sack, without moving, made me feel guilty. Those little fish looked so sad and dead that for a fleeting moment all the sadness of the world entered my heart, for everything has to die some day.

I apologised to the fishermen, but they just laughed and shrugged their shoulders, indifferent to my carelessness. I strode off to the moped, taking Mindi with me.

'Come on let's go.'

Mindi dug her heels in the sand and pulled me back.

'Sunset, sunset.'

Funnily enough I was no longer in the mood for glorious sunsets, empty beaches, or even emerald lagoons. I pointed firmly at the moped.

'We can watch it on the way back.'

Mindi followed. As I kick started the engine the fishermen waved. On the first kick the engine failed to start and the fishermen laughed. I cursed loudly and broke out into a sweat. Mindi put her arms around my waist, an act of impulsive intimacy that made me feel good.

'Eeh bar ting tong,' she whispered into my ear as mercifully, on the fourth attempt, the engine started.

We drove along the bumpy dirt track without speaking, the drone of the motorcycle dominating the atmosphere. Halfway up we encountered a group of six young travellers going in the opposite direction. The narrowness of the track forced us to stop and let them pass. As they did one of them asked if the track led to a beach and beautiful lagoon.

I thought about those fishermen wading in the sea, trawling their small net behind them, and their paltry catch in the white sack. They were working to put food in the bellies of their families, while these pampered Westerners were indulging selfish personal whimsies. As I tried to think of a good excuse to put them off, Mindi got in before me.

'Yah, no far an very beau-ti-ful!'

It wasn't Mindi's fault. She was just being herself, doing what the tourist industry had trained her to do, but as the travellers disappeared around a bend the realisation hit me hard, and with great clarity. It is pointless to go in search of new unspoilt destinations because even if you are the first, there will always be someone following close behind, and behind them somebody else, until eventually the deluge.

35.

After the rains abated the rock climbers and scuba divers returned to the islands, the rats disappeared down the drains, and even the ubiquitous mosquitoes were less in evidence. Once more all was quiet in Sang Som Town and business in the bar was non-existent.

Two days after the lagoon beach trip I was outside the bar, drinking a midday beer and reading the Bangkok post, catching up with news from back home and elsewhere in the world. It was the usual shit: death, war, famine, pestilence, terrorism. Pure snoozeville.

Mindi had gone to market and I was feeling good about things. Although business was slack the high season was only a couple of months away and, barring any major catastrophes, I reckoned we would hold out until then.

I supped my beer slowly, putting ice in to stop it going warm, and mused on the merits of moving on. My visa situation was suspect, the bar was just about making ends meet, and when it came right down to it I was getting bored, bored of the bar, bored of living with Mindi and bored of Sang Som town. The thrill was gone and I wondered vaguely how to break the news to Mindi and how she would react. I figured the best way was to break it gently.

As I sat outside the bar, lost in these thoughts, the Norwegian Orangutan appeared on the scene. He poked his head around a bamboo partition that separated his restaurant from the bar. He was in an unusually excited and agitated state.

'Have you heard the news?'

'What news?'

'Those filthy Muslims, it's their fault.'

'Pardon?'

The head continued to speak.

'Bombed Bali, that's what, lots of dead, all down to the evil Muslim, I hate Islam!'

The Norwegian's outburst didn't surprise me because he hated most things in life, but what he told was unsettling. According to him two bombs had exploded on the Indonesian island of Bali and over two hundred people, mostly Westerners, had been killed. The bombs had all the hallmarks of an Islamic terrorist attack. I pondered these facts for a few moments without saying anything.

'Do you not believe me?' screamed the head.

I did believe him, after all it had only been a year since 9/11 and the twin towers in America.

'Oi, there's no need to shout, I do believe you.'

The head wagged an ominous finger at me.

'Good, because this means business will be bad, not just for you, but for all of us.'

I resumed perusing the Bangkok post and thinking about more important matters like whether to have another beer because, unless you are directly involved, acts of terrorism are just drops in the ocean of eternity.

I was still reading the paper when Mindi returned from the market. She collapsed into a chair opposite and plopped her groceries down on a table.

'You drinking al-ready?'

'First of the day,' I lied.

Mindi slipped off her sandals and caressed her feet.

'There bomb in Bali.'

'I know, Norway told me, he reckons it will be bad for business.'

Mindi continued to rub her feet.

'I thing no, Bali far from Sang Som.'

36.

The next day a newspaper report of the atrocity appeared on the front page of the Bangkok Post. Two bombs had exploded on the paradise island of Bali. They had detonated in the tourist hotspot of Kuta, one hitting Paddy's Irish Bar and another larger bomb going off outside the Sari Club. Two hundred and two people had died as a result of the attacks. These disturbing facts put the event into sharp perspective. Some years previous I'd travelled through Bali and spent a few drunken nights in both bars. That could've been me, I thought worryingly.

It wasn't long before everyone in Sang Som was talking about the Bali tragedy. Everywhere you went the subject was discussed. Rumours began to circulate. Thailand was the next target: Bangkok, Phuket, Koh Samui, Sang Som. Any bar frequented by Westerners was a legitimate target. People got scared, paranoia struck and travellers changed plans, cancelled trips, and cut short holidays.

Western governments issued a series of warnings. They advised citizens against travel to places where fears of another terrorist attack like the one in Bali existed. And where did these fears exist? The U.S ambassador to Thailand clarified the situation.

'The Bali bombing in the middle of October must lead one to assume that no place is completely safe. The terrorists are sufficiently organised and sufficiently determined to try to carry out acts of terrorism anywhere in the world.'

More panic signals, more reasons to worry, more paranoia. As you can expect this statement didn't allay any concerns we may have been harbouring. To put it bluntly the news was depressing. Shortly after the attacks the tourist numbers in Sang Som fell by over forty percent, and we just didn't have the resources to survive another extended period of bad business. It was the final nail in the coffin of The Buddha Bar.

Once more we were inundated with long quiet evenings with nothing to do, but sit around and wait. Our problems revolved perpetually around money, or the lack of, and despite introducing another set of desperate cost-cutting measures, the bar once again struggled to stay afloat.

One cool night Mindi and I were on the rooftop drinking cocktails and discussing our troubles. I was listening and star gazing at the same time. It was a clear night and the stars were extra bright and captivating. As I tried to pick out a few recognisable constellations, I wondered about those stars. Why were they up there? What purpose did they serve? They didn't offend anyone, cause trouble, or let off bombs. They were just there for everyone's benefit, free of charge, gratis. And they were beautiful.

Mindi was still talking.

'What was that?' I said.

Mindi's look was sad and distant.

'You no hear Jo-Jo, you no listen, very important question.'

'What question?'

'I ask if can money flom England, help our bar?'

I had sensed the request coming for the last couple of weeks, and it must have taken a great deal for Mindi to bring it up, but I just didn't have any more money, home or abroad.

'Sorry, I don't think I can Min.'

Mindi's face flinched ever so slightly, but she said nothing more on the subject.

After this admission Mindi's demeanour underwent a negative transformation. She lost some of her old sparkle and, although reluctant to admit it, it was obvious she sensed the end was in sight. And to make matters worse even the girls sensed something was wrong.

One night, as we sat outside the bar waiting for customers to arrive, Nut spoke.

'Mister Jo-Jo, how bar do, no people?'

'Don't worry, everything will be okay,' I replied confidently and gave a phoney thumbs up sign.

Nut spoke to Pooh. They both smiled and I smiled back, but all our smiles were plastic ones. They were worried about their jobs and they had a right to be because we were in trouble.

Now the days and nights passed slowly and my thoughts constantly turned to home. I took to walking around the town in the early evening, pretending to be drumming up custom for the bar, but in reality I was loafing. Living and working in a failing bar was becoming claustrophobic and I needed some time on my own.

I wandered the streets of Sang Som, observing the scene, and explored the riverbank. I watched the river roll on out into the sea and cursed the people that had bombed Bali. I detested all forms of extremism. To my mind terrorism was an exercise in futility, but ultimately everything is an exercise in futility, because nothing really matters anyway. How could anyone kill a complete stranger in the name of a God, or democracy, or whatever? It seemed like humanity was deluding itself into taking things far too seriously, in a world spinning on a rotten axis?

37.

We were now officially desperate. Mindi's next great idea was a visit to the nearby Buddhist temple to make an offering to the Gods. Although a nominal Buddhist she rarely practiced the religion, hardly went to the temple, and abstained from meditation. And yet, at her core, the religion remained incredibly important in all aspects of everyday life.

Each morning, as the monks from a nearby temple made their early morning rounds, the townsfolk of Sang Som, in keeping with time honoured tradition, handed over offerings of food and drink. This was how the monks, who were forbidden to cook for themselves, got fed. Sometimes I'd be sitting outside the bar with Marvin, at the end of another marathon session, when a long row of monks in golden robes would suddenly materialise on the scene just as the sun rose in the East.

Now, with the bar's takings down to a trickle, Mindi decided it was time to get a little religion. She explained matters like this:

'Yah, we go Wat, make offering, incense, flowers, money, ba no money in this time, so we no money. An we pray to Lord Buddha for chok dee, this good luck in Thai. Our Lord Buddha always chok dee.'

So, on the day of a religious festival, off we went to the nearest temple to make our offerings to the holiest of holies. We took rice, flowers, incense, and a quantity of soft drinks from the bar's fridge.

'Monk love coke an sprite,' said Mindi by way of explanation.

At the temple, it was a crowded scene. As a procession of saffron robed monks passed by, scores of villagers handed over their offerings, and the more affluent the devotee the bigger and more grandiose the offering. There were no hymns, preachers, or any other formal sense of worship. Immediately I dug it.

'What do they do with all the food?' I asked Mindi, after we'd handed over our parcel of goodies.

'Eat for breakfast.'

'Seems a lot of food just for breakfast.'

'Other food save for last meal of day. No food waste. Give nuns or children who help round temple all time, an poor people who come temple mid-day.'

'Not a bad re-distribution of wealth.'

'Yah, any food left over give temple dog an cat.'

'And temple rat?'

'Eeh ba ting tong, come we back Buddha Bar, see if chok dee work an customer there any.'

38.

Three weeks after the bombing Marvin and I were sitting outside the bar in our usual positions. The impromptu visit to the temple had yielded little of any obvious chok dee and trade remained moribund. It was Saturday night and after ordering his third beer Marvin gave me the inevitable news.

'I'm leaving Sang Som.'

'Leaving?'

'On Monday.'

It wasn't an exaggeration to say Marvin was single-handedly keeping the bar afloat.

'Where ya gonna go?'

'Up North.'

'Chiang Mai?'

'Yep, Chiang Mai.'

I took a contemplative swig of beer and called for Mindi, breaking the news to her in a casual manner.

'Marvin is away to Chiang Mai on Monday and I think we should have a leaving party for him.'

Ever the pro Mindi concealed her disappointment and put on her best hostess face.

'Yah, we big par-ty you Marvin, Nicole, she come.'

At the mention of Nicole's name Marvin's eyes brightened.

'I would like that Mindi, d'ya know where she is?'

'Yah, she Phuket, I call her, she come an bring friend.'

Marvin glanced inside the empty bar.

'Yeah, could do with some other people, otherwise might be a boring party,' he said without a trace of sarcasm.

We held the leaving party for Marvin the following night. Mindi organised everything, buying streamers and party poppers, and even a small going away present. She also found an old sheet and designed a banner to hang outside the bar, on which were sewn the words, 'Goodbye Marvin & Chok Dee.'

During the preparations I was surplus to requirements and made a trip into town to see if I could find any random tourists to invite to the do. Maybe I hoped to rope some girls into coming so that Marvin might get lucky with one of them, or maybe I just wanted to go for a walk.

The streets were dusty and dead. I spent a fruitless afternoon on the lookout for groups of female tourists or any tourists. Eventually I gave up, sat on a wall at a crossroads, and watched some men at work. The men were plucking chickens and preparing them for market. I'd observed these men at work many times. They did the same shit every day, following a strict routine of plucking chickens, followed by cards and beer.

As I sat there worrying about my own perilous future, a salesman approached. We exchanged greetings, wai style, and he joined me on the wall. He was a Nepalese migrant who worked in a tailor's shop on the main street. The shop specialised in cut price made-to-measure suits sold exclusively to tourists. This fella's job was to get punters inside to buy the suits. He could speak several languages and his English was excellent, but working on a commission only basis, his livelihood as a tout was precarious at the best of times.

'How's business?' I asked

'Very bad, since Bali bomb, everything go downhill. How Buddha Bar?'

'Same,' I replied wearily, 'even thinking of going back West.'

'Back West, you mean England?'

'Yeah, I suppose, back to England and London.'

'Hey if go back, maybe take me with you.'

I laughed at that suggestion. People all over the world wanted to go to London and yet the attraction held little appeal. London just wasn't that good, and being poor there was just as bad as being poor someplace else.

'Forget London, why don't you go home?'

'I think you no understand, Thailand bad, Nepal hundred times worse.'

There was nothing I could say about that so instead I invited the tout to Marvin's leaving party, even promising him a free beer.

'Okay, I come when finish work,' the salesman said happily.

I stood up and wiped some accumulated sweat from my forehead.

'See ya later.'

'An don't forget my free beer,' he called out.

I walked off, raising my hand above my head, in a gesture of acknowledgement.

I strolled to the river and sat beside the pier. I gazed at the twin peaks of Khao Khnap Nam that guarded the entrance to Sang Som Town like natural colossi. Between the peaks a lone sea eagle soared and instantly I wanted to be transformed into an eagle, and soar like an eagle, and scour the land with my eagle eye.

A distant drone interrupted my bird of prey ruminations. Downriver a long-tail boat, its bow adorned with red strips of cloth, ploughed the green waters. When close enough I could see a group of travellers crammed either side of a huge mound of brightly coloured backpacks.

There were about twelve people aboard and they were all women, all young Western women. Girls. I jumped up and raced to the entrance of the pier.

As I waited for the backpackers to disembark, two young Thai boys appeared from nowhere. The lads were unofficial porters, on-hand to help travellers carry their backpacks, whether they wanted help or not.

These lads had a tactic. As the boatmen unloaded the baggage, they'd rush over and grab one, and then offer to carry it for the owner. If the bemused tourist refused assistance they would hold out their hand in hope of receiving some change. And if the owner refused to give any change they would level a volley of the filthiest abuse imaginable in the native language. I liked them, they had style.

I took a good look at the girls. A typical bunch of pre-university or gap-year students. They were mostly white and blonde, probably Dutch or South African. I was right more or less, because when they disembarked, the sound of harsh English accents informed me they were indeed from the land of Nelson Mandela.

Following the usual protocol I waited for the porters to do their business before approaching. The travellers probably had more important things to worry about than where to go for a drink, but in telling them about the bar I also handed out free tourist advice.

The girls seemed to appreciate this and their responses were warm and friendly. They were young and fresh, yet to become cynical and travel hardened, and in fact their natural exuberance rubbed off on me and I felt a surge of enthusiasm for the world.

Inspired, I made a point of talking to a pretty blonde girl, who immediately caught my eye. Short bobbed hair, fetching boyish looks, tanned skin, and young, maybe late teens. She wasn't tall, but perfectly proportioned, and dressed in a green vest with khaki shorts and yellow boots she looked like an action girl.

'So, is this a good bar?' said action girl.

'Are you joking, it's the best little bar in the world.'

39.

On my return to the bar I found Mindi, Nut and Pooh sitting outside eating sunflower seeds. I grabbed a bottle of beer from the fridge and stood in front of them.

'Invited quite a few people to the party,' I remarked in a self-satisfied tone.

'Yah?' replied Mindi sceptically.

'Yep, quite a few.'

Mindi glanced at my bottle of beer and then at the banner she had made for Marvin's leaving party. The banner lay folded on the table.

'After beer, wan you up put banner, wan there hang,' she said pointing to a space underneath the neon Buddha sign.

I put the beer down with some purpose.

'No time like the present.'

'You need ladder.'

I looked at the height of the sign. It was true I did need a ladder. Luckily, a few days before, I'd seen the orangutan fixing a spotlight with the aid of a lovely long wooden ladder.

'Norway's got one next door, I'll ask if I can borrow it.'

'Nasty old man won't help our bar, I know.'

'Let's see shall we.'

On entering his restaurant I found the orang-utan at a table. He was reading a newspaper and drinking a mug of tea. I told him my request straight off.

'Yo fella, do you have a ladder I could borrow please?'

'Yes, I have, you come with me.'

A little freaked by this unlikely cooperative attitude I followed. For the first time ever Norway was in good spirits, and when he offered to give me a hand putting up the banner, I figured he had just received a blow-job from the cleaner.

As we fetched the ladder the reason for the orangutan's cheerful disposition became apparent, but it had nothing to do with sexual favours from his employees, and more to do with world affairs.

'How's business?' he asked, as we carefully carried the ladder outside.

'Bad,' said I.

'Have you heard the good news?'

'What good news?'

'The Americans are to invade Iraq next year, probably the British also.'

'What's good about that?'

'Of course it's good news English. It means all those evil terrorists will get what's coming to them!'

At the bar Monkey boy asked if I had a hammer and nails. I walked into the bar and found a hammer and some nails. I handed the orangutan the hammer and a corner of the banner, and he put some nails in his mouth and climbed the ladder. I footed the ladder, holding it firmly with both hands.

'So what has invading Iraq got to do with terrorism?' I asked, as he pinned a corner of the banner to the underside of the neon sign. Norway took the nails out of his mouth before speaking.

'What do you mean? Iraq is where they are all trained, financed, indoctrinated.'

'Really?'

The Norwegian climbed down the ladder and we moved to the other side of the bar in crab fashion. He climbed up again.

'Personally, if it was down to me I would nuke the lot of them,' he said, as he banged in another nail and the banner went up.

'Nuke the lot of who?'

'All the Muslims, all the stinking oil rich Arabs that's who.'

'Hey, why don't we just nuke the whole world?' I said as we walked the ladder back inside his restaurant.

Norway slapped me on the back and laughed heartily.

'Ha, ha, you make joke, but can ask you one thing?'

'What's that?' I asked, hoping he wasn't going to ask me to kill any Muslims.

'The party, can you turn the music down after midnight, it keeps me awake up there on the roof.'

40.

When Marvin arrived at the bar on his moped he took one look at the sign, and smiled.

'You guys did that just for me,' he said.

I hand him a complimentary beer. 'Of course, you've been our best ever customer, and on top of that you're a likeable chap.'

Marvin took the beer and downed it in one gulp.

'Start as you mean to go on,' he burped.

From then on Marvin and I drunk steadily, working up a little beer buzz, while the girls kept an eye out for any potential customers. Yet, the streets of Sang Som were deadly quiet, like a Hollywood Western before a high noon shoot-out or a ghost town.

During the inactive interlude I told Marvin what the Norwegian man had said about America invading Iraq and asked for his opinion on the matter.

'Sounds like plenty of death,' he replied without hesitation.

That's what I liked about Marvin, he was a man of few words, but what he did say was choice.

We carried on drinking and talking. We talked about the so-called war on terror. Everyone agreed that if the U.S invaded Iraq it was because of oil. We couldn't find any other justifiable reason. It had to be over money, oil and political power.

Then the subject turned to religious intolerance. The girls were nominal Buddhists, but although they rarely practiced their religion they would not hear a bad word said about it. I turned to Mindi.

'The far South of Thailand has a large Muslim population, right?'

'Yah, Sang Som many Muslim people.'

'And do the Buddhists and Muslims get on together?'

'No, live like neighbour, sometimes same village, ba really no trust all time, an sometime kill.'

After a while the conversation dried up. The girls gossiped and me and Marvin supped slowly in the hot, humid, sticky evening. The streets remained empty, and apart from the drone of a distant moped, all was quiet. Then, just as Marvin's party was developing all the hallmarks of a wake, a large 4x4 appeared at the end of the dimly lit road like a beacon of hope.

The vehicle pulled up outside the bar. Everyone stopped talking. A tinted window wound down to reveal the smiling head of Nicole.

'Min,' she cried.

Nicole jumped out of the vehicle and embraced Mindi. Two middle aged white men stepped out of the vehicle. Immediately I recognised them, or thought I did. I scrutinised their faces. When Mindi saw the men, she let out a squeal of delight. There followed more hugging and kissing and over-familiar behaviour, which irritated me.

I was introduced to the two men. They were Americans and as we shook hands, I recalled where I'd seen them before. It was at the Golden Phallus bar during the kickboxing event on Pee Pee Island all those months ago. I wondered which one was shagging Nicole or even Mindi and an association of thoughts made me think about Karl and our time together, and I missed him.

With the arrival of Nicole the party finally got underway. Two Italian men appeared on the scene, followed shortly afterwards by my little Nepalese tailor. I played some samba music on the stereo while Mindi made Marvin a ridiculously huge cocktail complete with sparklers. Then Nicole handed over a card and present and gave him a great big kiss.

Everyone sat outside the bar drinking and talking. Marvin pulled out a bag of cough sweets.

'I haven't got a cough,' I said.

'Nor have I, but each sweet contains 10mg of codeine.'

I popped two cough sweets. They were green and had an apple flavour.

'I've got cherry flavour as well.'

I popped two cherry ones.

'If you take codeine with Valium you get a Percodan like effect,' said Marvin knowingly.

I didn't know what Percodan was, but took out a blue pill and popped it anyway.

'Marv, ain't you worried what all the pills and booze are doing to your health?'

'Yeah, a little, but in Chiang Mai I'm going to check into a Buddhist monastery for six months, total detoxification of mind and body.'

'Serious?'

'Totally serious.'

Mindi came over to our table.

'Jo-Jo, I go with Nicole an American men, you no mine?'

'Where ya going?'

'Yankee wan buy hotel an we know good one Ao Nang, you no mine I help?'

I decided I did mind.

'Don't you think you should be asking Marvin, I mean it's his leaving party after all?'

Mindi gave Marvin a hug.

'Marvin no mine, he just wanna dwink, anyway no we long.'

'Okay with me,' said Marvin.

I didn't say anything, but reckoned it was a liberty. Marvin had been our best ever customer and Mindi should have at least stuck around on his last night, but it was more than that. I'd also taken an instant dislike to the two middle-aged Americans with their big car, big waistlines and obvious wealth. Who did they think they were anyway? Fuck it and fuck them.

41.

After her shift ended Pooh went straight home, while Nut decided to stick around and hang out with the two Italian men. Strangely, the Italians were not drinking, the sort of behaviour that can send a struggling bar owner to an early grave. Yet, when I asked if they would like a drink, they firmly shook their heads the selfish bastards.

Marvin's leaving party was turning out to be a non-event and I blamed Mindi and Nicole.

'It doesn't matter,' slurred Marvin, after I'd moaned about them leaving for the third or fourth time, 'I frequent this bar because it's nice and quiet. If it was a busy bar I wouldn't have kept coming, coz there's nothing worse for the serious drinker in this world than a busy bar.'

This was a truism that couldn't be denied.

'I'll drink to that.'

As we raised our bottles some travellers appeared at the far end of the road. We watched as they approached. It was a large group of girls, and I was thrilled to recognise the South Africans from the pier. I gave them a wave.

'Hi everyone come on in, it's my mate's leaving party, but look he's all by himself and that's making him sad.'

Sitting all by himself Marvin did indeed look sad and lonely, even a little pathetic.

'That guy looks really depressed, let's cheer him up,' said a tall brown-haired girl.

As the girls discussed the merits of entering the bar I clocked the blonde girl I'd been so attracted to earlier that afternoon. When I caught her eye she smiled.

'Two drinks for the price of one,' I yelled crazily into the dead Sang Som night.

With that offer the girls tumbled into the bar like a human tsunami and their collective energy immediately brought Marvin's leaving party back from the brink of extinction. The bar was transformed from a sleepy half-forgotten backwater into a rocking private party. It was obvious the girls had been drinking beforehand because they were all in high spirits, even before taking advantage of my reckless 2-4-1 drinks madness.

With a party on my hands I became ultra energised and rushed around taking orders and serving drinks. I changed the music, found an 'Oldies But Goodies' compilation, flipped it on, and pressed shuffle mode. 'At the Hop' by Danny and the Juniors blasted out and immediately four South African girls began a spontaneous dance in front of the Buddha mural.

A couple of girls dragged Marvin from his usual spot and placed him firmly in the middle of what was by now an improvised dance floor. Then something remarkable happened. A man that only got out of his seat to go to the toilet commenced what can only describe as a crazed version of the funky chicken combined with the limbo.

'Who wants shots?' I cried out.

'How much?' cried the girls.

'I'm buying!' cried Marvin.

With that I poured twenty B52's and placed them on a tray. I handed the loaded tray to Nut, who paraded around the bar with it balancing on her head. A forest of hands rose up and within seconds the tray was empty. I found the streamers and party poppers and handed them around, and streamers streamed, and poppers popped, and now we were really swinging and jumping.

When Bare Footing by Robert Parker pumped out of the speakers I kicked off my sandals.

'Shoes off,' I cried

Shoes, flip-flops and sandals went flying, and everyone got down in a bare foot style, even the two sober Italian freaks.

For the next couple of hours everyone danced and drank and talked and shouted and made merry. With Mindi away I felt liberated. I'd been living like an old man, an old married man, and I was too young to be acting like that. As the party raged I managed to catch the eye of the blonde girl several times, and each time she smiled and my heart roared.

Now positive waves were everywhere and when 'Only You' by The Platters floated out of the speakers, the blonde swayed towards me. With my heart pounding she wrapped her arms around my neck.

'What's your name?'

'Marie and yours?'

'Joseph.'

'Joseph, Joseph, Judy, Judy, July, June, January.'

Marie was very drunk and stumbled a few times, but she was happy, just drunk with life and hope and love. She was young and I was young, and the night passed by in whirl of dancing and drinking. Before we knew it Marie's friends began leaving the bar, staggering home, yelling and crying into the immortal night.

Marvin was dancing with a tall brunette and when I caught his eye he gave me a soppy grin, and now the night seemed like a special night made for mad drunken passion. I took Marie outside. Mindi might return at any second and I didn't want to spoil the moment, or for the moment to end.

Did she want to go for a ride down to the river? Marie nodded and we jumped on Mindi's moped. She held me tight like she would never let go. As I kick started the engine Marvin stumbled out of the bar with the brunette.

'Where ya going?'

'Back to my hotel.'

Hallelujah! I shook Marvin's hand.

'Listen, just in case I don't see you before you leave, good luck in the Monastery and good luck in life.'

'Don't worry, you won't be getting rid of me that easily, I'll be back.'

Then, just as me and Marie pulled out of the lane, a familiar looking 4x4 appeared in front of us. The vehicles sudden emergence caused me to skid to an abrupt halt. A tinted window wound down and Mindi's angry head popped out.

'Where go?'

'Erm, I'm just taking this girl home.'

Mindi looked at Marie and Marie smiled and kissed my neck. Shit, I thought. Then Marie said hi, just about, and Mindi smiled falsely.

'Who looking our bar?'

146

'Nut.'

Mindi rolled her eyes.

'Nut?'

Nicole leaned over from the other seat.

'Where Marvin?'

'Went back to his room, too many beers.'

Nicole looked disappointed and Mindi shot me a quick look of death.

'Okay, take girl guesthouse, ba no long.'

I nodded, started the engine, and rode away. Not long? Okay. No it wasn't okay, and with the cool wind rushing through my hair I decided to take as long as I liked.

'Who was that?' Marie slurred into my ear.

'Oh, she owns the bar,' I said, but the engine drowned out my words and Marie clung on tight.

I parked the moped by the riverside. We gazed at the dark water rolling on by. I felt alive, like all my nerves were standing on end, my heartbeat fast and uneven. I was drunk and high, but perfectly in control. I saw the stars, blinking, flashing.

Marie turned to me. 'It's a beautiful night, a lovely, wonderful night.'

'The stars came out to play, just for us.'

It was a cheesy line, but I really meant it and because of that it sounded sincere and for Marie it was enough. Young and drunk, she wrapped her arms around me and our lips met, our mouths opened, and our tongues touched. I slipped a hand inside her shorts and she didn't pull away. I slipped another arm inside her vest and touched a pert breast and soft nipple, and she didn't pull away.

'Do you want to lie down?'

'Yes,' said Marie, and the stars burned and the river flowed. And as we lay together on the warm grassy riverbank the moon poked its head out from behind a passing cloud and knew everything. I closed my eyes.

When I awoke it was dark, but the darkness had less intensity than a few hours before. I checked the time on my watch. It was four thirty in the morning. I shook my head, saw Marie, and wondered.

I watched Marie sleeping for a while. She looked like a lost child and I was glad nothing had happened. It was good nothing had happened, but I had to steal a kiss as a memento of our night together. I kissed her cheek lightly and felt her warm, soft, uneven breath, and then she woke up.

At first Marie was disorientated and confused, looking at me like something foreign, an unknown quantity.

'Who are,' she whispered, but I cut her short.

'I'm Joseph from the Buddha Bar.'

Marie looked down at herself, checking to see if she had been violated. Instantly I read her mind.

'Don't worry, nothing happened, we just fell asleep.'

Marie breathed a sigh of relief.

'Oh thank god...'

The sigh and words bruised my ego.

'Oh I don't mean.....'

'Come on, let's get you back to your guesthouse, where ya staying?'

Marie pointed across the road to the hostel where Karl and I had stayed when we first arrived in Sang Som all those millions of years ago. It felt like my time in Sang Som had come full circle. I sat astride the moped and kick started the engine. Marie looked uncertain. Blushing bright red she jumped on the back of the moped, but this time she didn't hold me tight, and instead gripped the handrail. I rolled the bike over the road and Marie jumped off. We looked at each other.

'Hey, thanks for the dance.'

Marie held a finger to her lips.

'The dance?'

'Bye Marie.'

42.

After leaving Marie and the river behind my thoughts turned to Mindi and what her reaction to my disappearance might be. The town was just beginning to wake with shops opening and people moving here and there in the shadows of early morn.

I was energised, remains of alcohol coursing through my bloodstream, still kicking in. I'd tell Mindi I fell asleep by the riverside alone, hope she fell for it and crash out and forget everything.

At the bar all was quiet. The only signs of a party a few hours earlier were some party poppers and streamers that lay scattered on the ground like the remains of expended energy gone forever. Even Marvin's banner had fallen down and lay wrinkled sadly in a dusty corner. I crept inside feeling like a fugitive in my own home. I grabbed a cold beer, undid the top, and flicked the cap onto the floor.

At the DJ area the CD's lay in a jumbled pile. I rummaged through the pile until I located a Neil Young CD, turned the volume up, and flopped down on some cushions under the Buddha mural.

As the music played I thought of Marie and suddenly wished I'd fucked her by the riverside under the stars. And yet at the same time I was glad I hadn't. It wasn't meant to be.

Sometime later a stream of angry words roused me from my boozy slumbers.

'Eeh Joe bah ting tong!'

I looked up just as Mindi emerged from the shadows. She wore a traditional sarong, no make up, and looked more Asian than ever before. Her face was contorted in anger.

'Calm down,' I said.

'Where been?'

Where had I been? Best to get my story straight.

'I fell asleep down by the river,'

'No, possible, no possible!'

'Shut up!'

'You go with girl!'

'I didn't go with any girl, are you crazy?'

'No crazy, you lie!'

We started to argue. Accusations and denials filled the air. I was tired and hung over. At some point I made an attempt to get to the bedroom. Mindi barred the way. Things came to a head.

'Get out of my fucking way,' I shouted, and shoved Mindi so hard that she stumbled backwards and fell onto the kitchen floor. Shocked by my actions I rushed over to see how she was, but she pushed me away, wiping a hand across her mouth. There were spots of blood around her lip.

'Go from me,' she screamed.

On the bunker was a large knife we used to cut fruit for customer cocktails. We looked at the knife and then at each other, but before I had time to react Mindi grabbed the knife.

The situation was now officially ridiculous and I started laughing. Mindi didn't see what was funny. She screamed and lashed out with the knife. I threw my hands up and the blade sliced deep into the palm of my right hand. The contact between hand and blade didn't feel good. I looked down, a large piece of skin and flesh hung loose, with blood spurting out in thin red jets.

Mindi dropped the knife and screamed. I grabbed her with my good arm.

'Fetch me a fucking towel.'

Mindi rode me to the same hospital she had stayed in after the brutal attack by her husband. Once checked in they gave me a general anaesthetic. I awoke to find myself in one of the kennel like rooms, surrounded on all sides by oppressive navy blue curtain.

The injured hand was bandaged, but I couldn't feel any pain. Mindi was asleep in a chair. Tear tracks down both cheeks clearly visible.

I knew it was over and the adventure had finally come to an end. The bar was finished, doomed from the start, doomed to fail due to unforeseen circumstances beyond anyone's control.

Finally Mindi opened her large brown eyes.

'How are you?' I whispered.

'Jo-Jo I sorry, you bel...'

'Shut up, it was an accident, forget about it,' I pointed to my bandaged hand, 'how many stitches?'

Mindi rubbed her nose guiltily.

'Nurse, she say, thirty-nine.'

The amount impressed me. 'How much we have to pay?'

'We pay lot, you farang, pay more Thai people.'

'How much?'

'Ten thousand baht.'

'How did you get the money?'

'Use rent money, bar money, Jo-Jo now no money!'

'Min, I think it's over.'

Mindi squeezed my hand and surprised me.

'Yah, I thing same.'

For a few moments we didn't say anything, but when Mindi broke the silence it was to utter words that needed to be said.

'They wan you stay more night in hos-pi-tal, ba pay more.'

'How much?'

'Two thousand.'

I sat up and swung my legs off the bed.

'Come on, we're leaving.'

It was not a difficult decision.

43.

Back at the bar I felt weak and asked Mindi to buy some medicine, specifically requesting codeine and Valium. She returned later with generic acetaminophen and some generic diazepam. Armed with these I dosed myself up, drank a bottle of beer, and retired to my room and slept for twenty-four hours.

I awoke disorientated and my hand hurt. In the darkness of the stuffy room I pieced together the mad events of the previous 48hrs. Nothing made sense and my head felt like it was full of cotton wool. I popped another couple of acetaminophen and made my way shakily downstairs.

I grabbed a beer from the fridge and remembered to look at my watch. It was seven-thirty in the evening. The bar was silent, without music, and all the chairs and tables were missing. I walked through wondering where they were.

I found Mindi and Nicole sitting on empty beer crates outside the bar. On sensing my presence they looked up.

'You okay Jo-Jo?' asked Nicole.

I raised my bandaged hand like it was an injured bird wing.

'Yeah, I'm fine, what happened to all the tables and chairs?'

'Chinese lady wan rent,' explained Mindi in a resigned manner, 'I have pay, so sell chair an table my friend, good deal, my friend open bar Cha Fao Pier.'

'Good location,' I said absentmindedly, 'where are the girls?'

Mindi sighed wearily, an exhalation that hinted that life was too much even for her irrepressible nature. It was a bad vibration.

'Nut, she go Italian men, go Pee Pee Island. Pooh home, no customer an no money pay her.'

The girls' actions made perfect sense. Okay, I could have mentioned something about rats deserting a sinking ship, but in the circumstances it seemed inappropriate. Mindi and Nicole resumed a conspiratorial convo in Thai, and every so often shot concerned looks in my direction. They were planning something and I felt like the odd one out.

After a while the girls stopped talking. An oppressive silence descended. Nicole stood up awkwardly from a beer crate.

'I go now,' she said in a staged manner. She kissed me on the cheek, 'you careful Jo-Jo.'

She said something to Mindi in Thai and then departed the scene. Mindi gave me a hug and fluttered her long glossy eyelashes.

'You wan cocktail? I make best cocktail whole Sang Som?'

It was an offer impossible to turn down.

'Drink em on the rooftop.'

'Good tinking Spiderman!'

Despite everything, I laughed out loud at that one.

We sipped pina coladas, and gazed out over Sang Som, while Mindi explained the situation in an open and honest way. She was closing the bar and going to Phuket with Nicole and the two Americans. The Americans owned a hotel in Phuket and they wanted her to manage it.

'Jo-Jo, I leaving tomorrow.'

Situations can change rapidly. Mindi was only doing what she had to do to survive and it was the right move, a clean break, avoiding any long messy drawn out farewells.

'Good idea,' I said finally.

'Yes, I thing bess way, bess way both me you.'

I sipped my cocktail thoughtfully. Now all I had to worry about was numero uno. We stood in silence, each of us considering the future apart and more than likely in different parts of the world. Although I'd sensed it coming, it was still a shocker, and I laughed inwardly at the irony of the situation. All along I'd worried how to tell Mindi of my plans to leave, but when it came to the crunch she was leaving me.

'Jo-Jo, wha you do?'

I looked into those large black eyes, the same optics that had captivated me all those hazy months ago.

'I'm going home,' I said. And this time I really meant it.

'Yah, good idea, an when okay, you back Thai-land an come me Phuket.'

Somehow I didn't think so. This was the end. Another cycle of my life was over and a burning sixth sense told me I'd never see Mindi again.

Gradually and inevitably the conversation turned to the logistics of closing a business and tying up all loose ends. The landlady had given us a fortnight to vacate the premises. This was a lucky break and such generosity was good news, especially for me, because there would be time for my hand to heal. It also gave me time to think about my next move, even though I didn't have a clue what my next move would be. Mindi had sold the fridge, stereo, even the cooker.

'What about the Buddha sign?'

'No, my friend no wan, say bad luck.'

'Figures.'

Mindi generously offered to share the proceeds from sales of stock, but I declined the offer. I still had my return flight and two hundred U.S dollars squirrelled away in a backpack. It wasn't much, but it was enough.

'You keep it Min, it's all yours anyway.'

'Ba 2500 baht for fridge get,' she protested.

I gave her a big hug and took another swig of my cocktail. Mindi's eyes were big and bright and filled with tears.

'Promise visit soon me?'

'I promise.'

The next morning Mindi rose early and packed all her stuff. We ate breakfast, and at ten o'clock Nicole arrived with one of the Americans in the big shiny 4x4. The final farewell was a touching scene with hugs and kisses and promises to meet again filling the air. And then Mindi was away up the road and out of my life, just like that. All I had to do was blink and she was gone.

44.

The next day a man arrived and collected the bar's remaining stock. I helped him load the fridge, stereo and cooker onto the back of a truck, and waved him goodbye. Then I was on my own.

The only thing left in the bar was drink so I decided to drink it all, mixing spirits, and drinking whatever was to hand. I popped more pills and the days passed in a narcotic and alcoholic haze. I slept for long periods.

I found a pot of emulsion and spent an enjoyably therapeutic hour or two painting over the Buddha mural. Sometimes I took a ride into town and along the river and thought about all that had happened. My hand healed quickly. When able to move the fingers freely I booked myself on the first available flight out of Bangkok.

One evening I sat outside the now defunct bar with the Buddha sign on. I stared at the red neon. It seemed like my whole life had been one long dream, but now the dream had broken. I was going nowhere and the Buddha sign was a symbol of my lack of direction. After a while I switched it off. Mindi's friend was right, maybe it was bad luck.

And then Pooh showed up.

'Jo-Jo, you no go?'

I was smoking a cigarette and drinking a pint of Midori.

'Not yet.'

Pooh had come to collect the moped on behalf of Mindi. I gave her some money, asked her to return for the bike in two days, and told her not to tell Mindi that I was still in town.

'Jo-Jo, why no go?'

'Because I'm ting tong.'

'Yah, you ting tong.'

45.

The following morning I decided to go to the beach. I popped a couple of codeine pills, grabbed a bottle of Grand Marnier, and jumped on the moped. At the beach I found a desolate spot and gazed at the sea.

What was I going to do with the rest of my life? That was the burning question. I was young, but too old to be bumming around, shit I was nearly thirty. Anyway the world was changing and I didn't like what I saw. I picked up a pebble, threw it into the sea, and contemplated suicide.

I laughed at that crazy idea, a weird, almost hysterical laugh that lasted a good five minutes or so. The pills and booze were discouraging me, bamboozling my thinking processes, coating them in a thick layer of sludge. I took a swig of Grand Marnier and walked into the jungle.

A small river meandered seawards. The water was crystal clear. I jumped in, holding the bottle of Grand Marnier high above my head, and floated along the current. The water was refreshingly cool, sensual, and erotic. I floated past a section of muddy riverbank on which hundreds of strange looking crabs scuttled around.

Along with a normal sized pincer these crustaceans were armed with another huge salmon pink pincer, an extraordinary pincer. It was ridiculous, a cruel evolutionary joke, but the crabs didn't mind and waved them around incessantly.

What purpose did those giant pincers serve? I wasn't sure, but on closer inspection the crabs buried themselves in the grey mud and disappeared from view. I stopped floating. After a while the crabs re-emerged and recommenced waving their crazy claws around.

The sight of those funny crabs filled me with positive vibes. I jumped out of the river and ran back to the beach. I had to stop feeling sorry for myself and do something with my life. After all I could've have been born a crab with a freaky arm!

I rode back to the bar, packed my things, and got ready to say a final goodbye to Sang Som town. That night I wrote a letter to Mindi. It was a letter of apology because for the last few days, especially since her departure, I'd been consumed with guilt.

What was I doing pretending to be a businessman and part owner of a bar, when all along if the crazy venture failed England and the safety of home beckoned? What sort of a man was I? It had all been a big game, an excuse for one long extended party, but for Mindi it had been everything, her reason for living, and hope for a better life.

But maybe it wasn't my fault. Maybe it wasn't anybody's fault, not me, not Karl, not Mindi, not anyone. My emotions were mixed up and I began to cry. Soon the letter was splashed with tears and the ink smudged, and the words blurred. Then the alcohol got to me. I crashed out on the floor, in front of where the Buddha mural had once gazed down upon days and nights in the life and death of a small bar in Southern Thailand.

I awoke with a raging hangover and re-read the letter with trembling hands. None of it made sense, pure gobbley-gook. I screwed the letter up and threw it down the drain. I took my prescribed drugs and threw them down the drain, along with the rest of the alcohol. The time had come to clean up my act.

When ready to depart I locked the bar, left the keys of the moped in the ignition, and caught a taxi to the bus station. As the bike rode along the busy streets of Sang Som I made sure not to look back, not even once, because when you're leaving a place forever you can never look back...

Photograph © by Amber Ace

About the Author

Joseph Ridgwell was raised in East London and is a cult figure of the literary underground both in the UK and abroad. He has published five collections of poetry, two short story collections, three novellas and one novel.

Ridgwell Stories was nominated for a 2016 Pushcart Prize and longlisted for the 2016 Saboteur awards.

A 6th collection of poetry - *Cosmic Gigantic Flywheel* - is due to be published in 2018 by Lenka Editions in Paris.

A 7th Collection of poetry - *The Beach Poems* - will be published by New York's Bottle of Smoke Press in the summer of 2018.

Ridgwell's work has also appeared in numerous anthologies.

For further details of the authors work and current state of mind go to his website: http://josephridgwelljr.wordpress.com/

COLOPHON

This second edition of *The Buddha Bar* was published in May 2018 by Ternary Editions. Designed and typeset by Bill Roberts in North Salem, NY. The text is set in Adobe Caslon Pro.